My Not-So Rad Afterlife

Shannen Camp

D1522456

ISBN: 9798858581710

Cover design: Sugar Coated Covers
Cover images: Shutterstock
Fonts: Copyright © 2023 GGBotNet (https://ggbot.net/fonts),
with Reserved Font Name "Third Street".
Typeset by: Shannen Camp
Edited by: Cookie Lynn Publishing

DEDICATION

For Serena. Who fixed my creativity when it was broken.

And for 90s pop culture. I'll always love you.

Also, Taika Waititi. You know what you did.

My Not-So Rad Afterlife

Chapter 1

I sat on the dining room table, tucked comfortably between the roast beef and rolls. The diners around me silently pushed their food around on their plates. They all looked a bit sullen since the night had been relatively uneventful. Everyone was waiting for me to do something. The family who owned the home had even invited their friends over for the show because, as the mother of the house put it, "Trish thinks she's so high and mighty with her goat yoga and her gluten-free brownies, but wait until she sees what we've got."

And still I hadn't done anything all night. Mostly because I sort of enjoyed watching the uncomfortable tension at the dinner table. I had the ideal viewing spot sitting cross-legged right smack dab in the middle of the table with my chin in my hand.

But enough was enough. These people had come here to see something, and I wasn't going to disappoint.

Well... I was going to disappoint just a bit. Because instead of going full-blown poltergeist, I'd just move a few things around. Maybe create a cold spot or two. If Trish-the-annoying-next-door-neighbor really got on my nerves, maybe I'd pull her hair. But that was it.

Nothing too flashy.

Straightening my posture and tilting my head from side

to side to crack my neck, I placed my pointer finger on the salt shaker beside me and gave it a small push. It scooted about an inch across the table, but you'd think I had blasted an air horn.

Everyone at the table inhaled at once, staring intently at the salt shaker. I gave myself a satisfied smile and glanced over at Trish. "Boo-yah, lady. How do you like me now?"

She looked… bored? She crossed her arms, and—I kid you not—she had the audacity to yawn. And not a subtle yawn where you try to keep your mouth closed to be polite but end up getting super watery eyes because of your effort. She literally put her hand over her mouth just enough for me to see she was full-on yawning.

"Seriously, Trish?"

Of course, she couldn't hear me, but that didn't lessen my indignation.

Taking a deep breath to calm myself, I pushed the salt shaker a few more inches, slowly enough to make sure Trish saw.

She had.

She was watching it with the same bored expression while the rest of the dinner guests looked like they might pass out.

And then, slowly, deliberately, and annoyingly, Trish turned to the hostess who had put this whole neighbor dinner together. "You know salt is really bad for you, right?"

"That's it," I said, throwing my hands into the air and jumping off of the table. "Salt is really bad for you," I mimicked in my most unflattering voice. "I'll show her what's bad for her."

Walking up behind Trish's chair, I grabbed it and pulled it out a good foot away from the table, bringing Trish with it. She gasped and grabbed the arm rests before trying to collect herself. She gave a nervous little laugh. "Fun trick."

"Trick, Trish? Really? As if." I was so done with this lady. "I think it's time for you to leave. The Newman's can do *so* much better in the friend department."

I didn't bother with subtlety anymore. I dragged Trish's chair the length of the room to where the front door was, opened said door, and dumped her outside.

"Bye, Trish," I said with a wave, slamming the door behind me. "Fun trick," I scoffed with a shake of my head, stalking back to the dining room.

Most of the dinner guests ran toward the front door to make sure the annoying neighbor was okay, while some sat in shocked silence. I shouldn't let one bad apple ruin the entire evening. I'd still managed to scare a few people, so the day wasn't a total waste. But it could have been so much better than it was. I hated having to be so obvious.

Sighing, I gave one last long look around the room at all the subtle things I had planned for the evening. I pulled myself from the room, popping into the old, abandoned house in Ramona where I liked to stay when I wasn't scaring the life out of people.

People in Ramona, California were relatively laid back. They had their horses. They kept to themselves. They were all scared of the house I'd made my own because it was supposedly haunted.

I mean… I guess it was *technically* haunted, since my friend and I sort of lived there.

Lived there? Remained dead there? After-lived there? I had no idea what the proper terminology was. This wasn't one of those things I could look up on the world wide web.

Sitting down on the roof of the house in the warm Southern California night air, I tugged on my black velvet choker with the pewter butterfly hanging from it. It was sort of like a comfort blanket. That and my smiley face ring. I couldn't take everything with me from my living days, but somehow, Jojo, who ran the afterlife, knew I needed those two things.

"Someone was a mega drama queen tonight," a familiar voice said.

"Oh geez," I answered, putting my head in my hands before I even saw her. "It's not on the news, is it?"

3

"Jane, I love you, but no one actually watches the news anymore. You know that, right?" Jenny sat next to me, taking off her fedora.

"Where did you see it?"

"Social media, girl. This isn't the 90s. We don't use dial-up to access whatever weird texting service you used back in your day," she said.

"A.i.m."

"What?"

"A.O.L. Instant Messenger," I corrected. "It was the cool thing. You'd log into a chat room and ask for people's A/S/L."

"A/S/L?" she asked, though she didn't look too invested in the conversation.

"Age, sex, location."

"Wow... so in the 90s people were just asking to be murdered?" she asked, her voice full of sarcasm.

"Murder at the speed of dial-up."

"Yeah... we definitely don't use that."

I rolled my eyes. "You have to stop saying 'we' like you're still alive. Your 'we' is officially the post-millennial generation you are no longer a part of."

"Man, I thought you'd be in a better mood after throwing that chick out of her house. Apparently you're just cranky tonight." Jenny's gaze floated to her phone.

She couldn't actually use the phone for anything useful, but she couldn't seem to put it down. Just like my choker and cheap ring I'd gotten out of a quarter machine, Jenny's phone was her comfort item she'd brought to the other side. Or maybe it was considered the middle since "other side" suggested there were only two sides to life instead of however many there actually were.

The big cosmic joke on everyone was the fact that, even in death, you still have absolutely zero idea what's going on in the grand scheme of things. You know you get assigned to an area to haunt. You know some people become ghosts while others "move on," and you know ghosts can also "move on" eventually to whatever comes after this. Death after death or something. And even that might not be the final state. It might be another step in a never-ending procession of stages of eternity.

Oh, and you also knew Jojo, a middle-aged Kiwi guy with the weirdest sense of humor I'd ever seen, was in charge of all the ghosts and their haunting assignments.

It was hard not to be grumpy when you didn't exactly know where you came from or where you were going or why you were here. I guess those really had been good questions to ask in life. Except that they still weren't answered in death.

"How was your night?" I asked Jenny, wanting to change the subject.

Jenny played with one of her dark curls and kept her phone in front of her. "It was good. Just slammed a few doors and stole a few socks."

This made me smile a bit. At least one question had been answered in death. It was almost like afterlife hazing to steal just one sock from people's laundry. It was a petty trick, but we couldn't just let a tradition that had been going on for ages die out with us. We didn't need another reason for past generations to hate us.

"From the cute boy?" I asked, nudging her with my shoulder.

She grinned and popped her gum a few times but didn't answer.

"I'll take that as a yes."

"Girl, he is so hot," she said, fanning herself for effect. "And I am like... a national treasure. He should be honored to have his socks stolen by me. Like, this is a privilege, and he doesn't even know it."

Jenny had this kind of nasally quality to her voice that almost made it sound like she was whining all the time. At first, I'd found it annoying, but since she was my best friend in this afterlife, for better or worse, it had become endearing. That and

5

My Not-So Rad Afterlife

the way she talked, which was always full of exaggeration and drama... I sort of loved it.

"He should be bragging to his friends about how honored he is," I agreed, still smiling.

"Speaking of boy toys, shouldn't you be watching your man on TV right now?" Jenny asked. "What's his name? Brooding Ghostface or something?"

"Brody Specter," I corrected. Jenny gave me a meaningful look. "Okay, fine, it's a stupid stage name, but he's so good at what he does. It's like art watching him work."

"He literally just goes to old smelly houses and asks how people died. And then he says he can feel their presence. It's kind of a terrible excuse for night time television."

"He's a paranormal investigator. That's what they do." I knew she was right. It was kind of cheesy the way they did things on the show Brody was on, but he had to be over-the-top for the cameras. It was a ratings thing, not a Brody thing.

"Whatevs, girl. Go get your man," she said, shooting me a thumbs up.

I gave her a mock salute and made my way to the Johnston's house.

Chapter 2

Adam and Rita Johnston were a newlywed couple in their twenties who watched *The Specter Files* religiously. Every Wednesday night at eight o'clock, I knew I could find Brody Specter. The Johnstons finished dinner by six, made some cookies, and by eight PM sharp, they were on their living room couch, curled up under a blanket, and ready to start our favorite show.

It was nice to find people so predictable. It meant I never had to miss an episode of my favorite paranormal investigator. I had a massive crush on Brody Specter. The fact that his entire job was trying to contact ghosts made me feel like we had this sort of Romeo and Juliet relationship. It was a nice little fantasy.

"Hello Johnstons," I said, walking through the closed front door and finding a comfy spot on the loveseat beside their sofa. "Have a good week?"

They didn't answer me, obviously, but it still felt nice to talk to them. It made it feel less like I was invading their privacy.

If I was haunting them, it wouldn't feel weird at all. But these were just some nice kids I had decided to mooch off of. I didn't want to make it weird.

"I got a sale at work today," Adam said to his wife.

"Nice work, Adam," I said, keeping my eyes on the TV

screen as the intro to *The Specter Files* began playing.

His wife said something in response, but I was already in the zone.

"Investigating the Overlook Hotel?" I asked, giving a low whistle to show how impressed I was. Last week he'd investigated The Winchester Mystery House, which I would totally kill to haunt, but couldn't because it was technically in Northern California, which was out of my region. "Johnstons, can you keep it down?" I added to the couple, who were still talking.

They hadn't heard me, but they stopped talking as if they had, which I appreciated.

And there he was. Brody Specter. Wearing his signature black jacket and jeans. Geez, he was good looking.

I let myself adopt a dopey smile while I watched him wandering down darkened hallways with just a flashlight and a video camera. He really needed to investigate somewhere in Southern California so I could pay him a little visit. Maybe if I got his attention, we could somehow work through this whole I'm-dead-and-he's-not thing. If anyone would understand, it would be Brody Specter.

The Johnstons were both completely silent as we all watched the show with baited breath. It was funny to watch a show about ghosts now that I was one, but somehow, it was still scary. Even knowing that some random person like me was behind all the "hauntings."

The best was when they said it was the ghost of some specific person haunting a historic site. Especially because I enjoyed recreating famous reports of paranormal activity, just to keep some of the old legends alive. It looked like I wasn't alone.

A loud bang from the other room made all three of us gasp at the same time. I would have been embarrassed by my reaction if Jenny had been around, since, as a ghost, I probably shouldn't get startled. But she wasn't there, so I didn't bother dropping my hand from my chest.

Rita and I looked at Adam, waiting for him to get up to

investigate, even though I easily could have checked it out myself.

I really hoped it wasn't an intruder.

I liked the Johnstons. I couldn't let anything happen to them. And I wasn't sure it was allowed for me to take matters into my own hands when it came to altering the course of fate or whatever.

"Probably just the wind," Adam said, getting up and slowly making his way to the other room. Rita and I followed close behind.

Even though I was worried about what we'd find, it was kind of nice, feeling like I was one of the living again. Even if it was only for a second.

When Adam rounded the corner, he let out a sigh of relief. "It was a book." He picked up the offending book and showed us. Well, he showed Rita. I just happened to be standing beside her. "It fell."

"What made it fall?" she asked, still looking a bit terrified.

"Yeah, Adam. What made it fall?" I asked.

"Probably a ghost," Adam responded, his voice adopting an air of drama as he dropped the book, tickled his wife, and followed her to the couch to continue watching their show.

I stayed in the room where the book had fallen and did a slow scan, making sure there wasn't some armed robber the Johnstons hadn't seen. I didn't care if I would be breaking the rules. If someone tried to kill this family, I would definitely have to step in and scare them to death. It seemed only fair.

"Yeah, that's right," I said to the empty room, trying to sound tough. "You back off my family. This is *my* turf."

I pointed at the empty room with narrowed eyes, to make sure it really understood.

"I wasn't aware that this family was taken," a voice said in the darkness, making me fall backward onto the floor.

I backed away from the voice on the heels of my hands until my back hit the wall, dislodging another book from the shelf. I wasn't great at controlling my ability to interact with the world around me when I was scared. "W-who's there?"

"Are you... scared of me?" A man stepped from the shadows. "You can't really tell me you're scared of ghosts. You *are* a ghost."

I stood up as gracefully as I could and dusted myself off... even though I was a ghost, which meant I didn't actually get dusty. Ghost perk. "Psh," I scoffed. "As if."

The man raised a skeptical eyebrow.

"I was being ironic," I lied. "Duh."

I wasn't being ironic. He had nearly scared the black sunflower dress right off of me. But he didn't need to know that. He looked a bit smug already.

"Oh, 90s kids. The kings of irony," he said. "Never mind that none of you actually know what irony is. You know Alanis Morissette got it wrong, don't you? Which is, in and of itself, a bit ironic."

I pointed a finger at the ghost in front of me with his stupid gray tailored suit. "Never insult Alanis in front of me," I warned. "Alanis is sacred."

"I see I crossed a line." He raised his hands in surrender. "I apologize. I won't insult Alanis ever again."

"That's more like it," I answered, now walking in circles around him to size him up. "So, you're clearly not a new ghost, judging by your clothes."

"Well spotted," he said. "Although I could have died at a costume party."

I gave him a look that said I wasn't buying it. "If all those BBC movies taught me anything, I'd put you in the 1800s somewhere. Am I close?"

"Close?" he asked. "Well, when you give me a vague 100-year period, I'd hope you were close."

"Just answer the question," I said, exasperation in my voice.

"I died in 1861," he said.

"Victorian era?" I gave an impressed nod. "Nice. Very

classy. Accent is a nice touch."

"Yes, well, I live to serve," he deadpanned.

Was everything a deadpan when you were dead? Or was that just the kind of joke a dead dad would make?

"Anyway, I'm sort of... working this house, so... I need you to leave my people alone," I said, now coming to a stop in front of him. Hopefully, my circling technique had intimidated him. "So..." I let my request hang in the air.

"I don't see anywhere you've been assigned to this house," he said, his voice still slightly bored by our whole conversation. Maybe it was the British accent, but he definitely sounded like he was being condescending.

Sure, he had been dead longer than me. But it wasn't like I had died yesterday. I'd been haunting for two decades now. I was no amateur.

"Well... I'm not officially haunting this house," I backtracked. "But these people are still mine."

"Have you spoken to Jojo about this?" he asked. The name "Jojo" sounded funny coming out of a British person's mouth. The name wasn't nearly proper enough for the accent.

"I don't need to talk to Jojo about everything," I said, sounding much more defiant than I felt.

Jojo was in charge of everything. Or, at least, he was in charge of everything at this stage of death. Apparently, there was a big "high up" in the next-next life. But it was still a mystery. It was also a mystery how many "afterlives" you had to deal with before getting to the final one.

"I believe you *do* need to talk to Jojo about everything. He is, after all, the head honcho here, is he not?"

"The dead honcho," I snorted.

The British ghost in front of me didn't laugh. He didn't even crack a smile.

"Tough crowd," I said in my best Steve Urkel impression.

"Quite," was all the stuffy ghost said.

An awkward silence extended between us for a few

moments before I cleared my throat and played with my black velvet choker. "All right. Well, this has been fun. I'm glad we had this talk. Thanks for relinquishing the Johnstons back to me. And... no hard feelings, buddy."

Giving the man a smile and small salute, I pulled myself out of the Johnston's house before he could answer. I didn't want to give him the chance to argue. Appearing in the abandoned house in Ramona, Jenny was in the empty living room, taking selfies she wouldn't actually be able to send to anyone.

I snuck into my unofficial room and sat on the old bed there. Hopefully, this Victorian ghost wouldn't question my right to haunt the Johnston house. I really liked that couple. Plus, they never missed an episode of *The Specter Files*. Where else would I find that level of consistency?

I was confident I had made myself clear. That ghost wouldn't be back.

"Yeah, I'm gonna need you to leave the Johnstons alone," said a voice from right beside me, scaring me for the second time that night.

Apparently, the Victorian ghost was a snitch.

"Hi, Jojo."

Chapter 3

"What's up, sister?" Jojo asked in his thick New Zealand accent. "That's something you kids say, right?"

"I'm hardly a kid," I said, trying not to worry about the fact that Jojo had paid me a personal visit. That couldn't be a good sign. Was I about to be fired from the afterlife?

"What's like… the cool 90s slang? Da bomb? Are you da bomb?"

"Jojo, please," I begged. "Even 90s kids knew that phrase was a bad idea."

"Right. Talk to the hand," he said.

Jojo had died way back in the 1300s and had then been put in charge of this part of the afterlife. No one really knew who had been in charge before that or why they'd been fired, but Jojo had been the boss for centuries.

You would think a centuries old ghost would be dignified and serious, but Jojo was the exact opposite of that. He had died when he was forty-five but looked remarkably good for his age. He had tan skin, gray curly hair that he styled in a kind of pompadour, a gray five o'clock shadow, and a thick Kiwi accent. And unlike the rest of us, he wasn't stuck in the clothes he was wearing when he died.

Instead, he took his favorite pieces of clothing from each era and put them together in the most nonsensical outfits possible. Today he wore some early-2000s black skinny jeans with a neon green windbreaker from the 1980s and some black dress shoes that looked like they belonged to the Victorian ghost I'd run into earlier.

"Am I fired?" I asked Jojo, figuring it would be better to cut to the chase.

"Fired?" He laughed. "You know I don't care if you actually do your job or not, right?"

"You don't?" I found that hard to believe.

"Actually, I do. I don't know why I said that. Wanted to sound cool. I actually care very much if you do your job. That's why I'm here."

"I know I'm not technically assigned to the Johnston house, but I really like that couple. Isn't there any way that Victorian ghost can go haunt someone else? I could trade him for one of my other families," I suggested.

"Sorry kid, the Johnstons belong to William. And since he was recently assigned to this area, he needs all the families he can get."

"Come on, Jojo! You know that's such crap. Who makes these assignments?" I asked.

"The big man upstairs," he said.

"God?" I asked, wondering if Jojo might know what happened after this section of the afterlife.

"What? No. Richard Green in the labor management department," he answered, giving me a look like I really had died yesterday.

I stared at Jojo for a moment before responding. "I can never tell if you're joking or not."

"Serious as a heart attack, I'm afraid." Jojo crossed his legs on the bed beside me so that he was sitting criss-cross applesauce. He began picking at a stray thread on his skinny jeans.

"I'm surprised you can even cross your legs with your pants so tight," I said, trying not to be annoyed that I was losing the Johnstons.

"Ghost skills." He shrugged. "Anyway, just had to let you know you aren't allowed to haunt the Johnstons anymore without getting the A-okay from William first."

"Is William the smug, fancy British ghost?"

"Smug, fancy British ghost... I like that. I'm going to start calling him that. I had just been calling him Romeo boy for the past hundred years, thinking that was a clever William Shakespeare joke, but I like yours way better," Jojo said. "And yes. That would be him."

Jojo unfolded his legs and hopped off the bed, shaking his feet as if they'd fallen asleep.

"We all straight now?" he asked. "You'll stay away from the Johnstons unless William gives you permission to encroach on his turf?"

"Fine," I mumbled.

"That's the spirit!" he said with a clap. "Oh, and I heard about what you did at the Newman home this evening. Really great stuff. Nearly scared that suburban woman to death. Keep up the good work."

"I'll do my best, Jojo," I said, attempting to give him a halfhearted smile. As annoyed as I was by the news he'd delivered, it was impossible to stay mad at Jojo.

"All right, cool," he turned away from me as if he'd disappear, but instead he froze and turned back to me with a concerned look on his face. "Do these skinny jeans make my hips look too big?"

He did a little spin in front of me. He was a tall, skinny guy. I was pretty sure he'd never looked fat in his entire afterlife.

"You look great," I promised. "It's a good fit for you."

"That's what I like to hear." He turned and shouted to no one, "See, Richard Green from labor management! I *can* pull off skinny jeans." Then he turned back to me. "Jerk said I couldn't do it."

"The audacity," I answered with a slow shake of my head.

"I know, right?" he asked, before disappearing from

before my eyes.

It didn't matter how many times I'd seen other ghosts appear and disappear, it was always a little jarring to see someone dematerialize right in front of my eyes.

I wasn't sure I'd ever get used to it.

"Was that Jojo?" Jenny walked in and looked around.

"I got in trouble." I pouted.

"Girl, you better not piss him off. I don't want to find another roommate. All the other dead people straight up *suuuuuuck*."

"I don't know if anyone could piss Jojo off. He's like... the most easygoing dead person ever."

"Truth. But I still wouldn't test him." She was still typing away on her phone. You'd think after a few years of being dead, she would have broken that habit. "So, what did he want?"

I sighed, feeling supremely sorry for myself. "I have one week to suck up to a smug British ghost so I can watch my TV show."

Jenny's brow furrowed. "How much did I miss?"

"A lot," I confirmed. "Wish me luck."

Chapter 4

The Johnstons were asleep by the time I got to their house. I wasn't sure if William would still be there or if he'd be off haunting some other family by now. But since I didn't know who else he haunted, this was the only place I knew I could reach him. Plus, I really didn't feel like calling Jojo up to ask for this guy's contact info. Jenny was right. I didn't want to push my luck with the man in charge.

The Johnston home was dark as I walked through the deserted hallway toward the bedrooms. The couple was sound asleep with Adam snoring while Rita nudged him in annoyance every few minutes. There was no sign of William, so I made my way to the living room.

The TV was off, and I was half tempted to turn it on to see if there were any reruns of *The Specter Files* playing. But I wasn't allowed to do that since it would technically count as a haunting.

I stared forlornly at the TV. I definitely had a problem. That stupid reality show wasn't even that good. It just had a super-hot ghost hunter on it. When you were dead, it was the little things that mattered.

"I thought Jojo spoke to you," the British ghost said from somewhere in the kitchen.

He emerged from the darkness in his Victorian clothes,

looking like what I'd expect a ghost to look like. Ghosts from cool time periods had it made. They could just appear in front of their assigned households if they really wanted to scare someone.

If I tried to pull that stunt, no one would be scared. They would all wonder why some random girl in a sunflower dress and combat boots had shown up in their house. The prime of my life hadn't exactly lent itself to a spooky aesthetic. If I had been a bit more grunge back in my day, maybe I could have been scarier in the afterlife.

Since I didn't have my clothes to rely on for scares, I stuck to the subtle tricks. A cold breeze here, a knocked over object there; that was my wheelhouse. My personal favorite thing to do was open all the kitchen cupboards right after someone left the room. It always got a great reaction.

William stood watching me expectantly, looking like he could scare a room of teenagers without even trying.

"Jojo and I had a nice chat," I said, trying to sound nicer than I had the first time I'd spoken to him.

"And?"

"And I realize I was a bit rude to you earlier," I said. I needed to start majorly sucking up to this guy if I wanted to get his permission to haunt the Johnstons before next week's episode of *The Specter Files*.

I considered coming right out and telling him why I needed to haunt this house, but he didn't look like the type who cared about ghost hunting shows. He seemed too dignified for that sort of thing.

"I'm sorry I got so mad at you for haunting the Johnstons," I said evenly. "I'm a bit protective of this family."

William's eyes suddenly widened, and he looked almost sympathetic to my plight. "Oh dear. I'm so sorry. I didn't realize this was your *actual* family," he said.

I considered lying for a moment, but I knew he could easily find out the truth and then he'd never let me back in the house.

"Sorry... I worded that confusingly. They aren't *my* family. I just like them... as people."

"I'm not sure I follow," he said, his brow now furrowed.

"Here's the dealio," I said, biting the bullet and deciding honesty was the best policy. "The Johnstons watch *The Specter Files* every week, and it's my favorite show. I need a place to come watch, and they're... consistent."

William kept his brow furrowed. I couldn't tell if he was studying me or if he'd glitched out of the Matrix or something.

"You're serious?" he asked. "Jojo didn't tell you to come up with some ridiculous story as a hazing ritual for my new assignment?"

"Why is it so hard to believe I'd want to watch a show with some nice people?" I asked.

"I don't find that part hard to believe," he said, still looking like I was an alien instead of a ghost. "But *that* show? It's so kitschy and awful."

"It most certainly is not," I responded, indignation heavy in my voice. Apparently, I'd forgotten that I was supposed to be buttering him up.

"Oh, come on. That dreadful host walking around in houses and saying he 'senses a presence' when there's clearly nothing there? It's embarrassing."

"Brody Specter is an artist in his field," I said. "He studied parapsychology."

"That's not a real thing," William scoffed.

"You're a ghost!" I practically shouted. "How can you not think that's a real thing?"

"I could say the same of you. You're a ghost. How can you believe any of his methods are actually effective in contacting spirits? The man is a charlatan."

I pursed my lips. "I'm going to ignore the last few minutes and start over." My voice was even but threatened to break back into indignation at any moment. "Can I please continue to visit the Johnston home so I can watch *The Specter Files* with them?"

William still looked aghast at the fact that I enjoyed the reality show. In my defense, reality TV had been the hot new thing when I was alive. It was still somewhat of a novelty to me.

I didn't expect some stuffy Victorian ghost to understand its appeal.

"What do I get out of it?" he asked.

I raised my eyebrows.

"Um... what do you want? You can have any of my families."

He shook his head. "I've been on the Southern California circuit for a few months now. I have a few families, but I really like this new addition. You can come and see them once a week to watch your show under one condition."

"Name it." I would do pretty much anything for my one guilty pleasure.

"Will you show me around the region? Some of your favorite haunts, unique places to visit... that sort of thing. This is my first time haunting overseas, and it would be nice to have a native show me around."

"Really? That's it?" I asked, wondering if there was a catch.

"That's it."

"Done!" This was great! I wouldn't have to find another couple with my taste in TV programs. I could keep visiting the Johnstsons.

This was especially important since they'd been watching reruns of *Friends,* and I'd died before seeing the finale. I'd finally get to watch it if William really let me stick around.

"What does your evening look like tomorrow?" he asked.

Everything he said sounded so proper and stilted. I wasn't sure if it was just the accent, the time period he'd lived in, or his personality, but he'd need to loosen up a bit. He was haunting in Southern California now, not England.

"My evening is wide open," I answered, finally giving him a genuine smile.

This might actually be fun.

Chapter 5

"So… you're going on a *date*?" Jenny seemed much too excited for something that definitely wasn't a date.

"You do realize I'm dead, right? Dead people don't date."

"Speak for yourself, girl," she retorted. "I'm not letting my death keep me out of the dating scene. That would be a crime against humanity."

"As if. Who have you dated since you've died?" I asked.

She raised her eyebrows as if I'd challenged her to a duel. "There was that Russian Tsar from some old timey century," she said, beginning to count her conquests out on her fingers. "Plus, that French mime. There was that guy who was in some boy band from your time period—"

"First of all, his name is John Lennon. Second, he's not from my time period, because I'm not that old. And third, you didn't date him. It was some ghost with long hair and glasses who told you he was John Lennon. He was lying."

Jenny continued talking as if she hadn't even heard me.

"There was the bodybuilder, the marine biologist, the super-hot priest, and a few others I can't even remember right now."

"Touché," I answered.

I hadn't actually expected her to have a whole backlist of dead people in her arsenal. I guess Jenny didn't mess around when it came to proving someone wrong.

"So yes, this is a date," she concluded. "But I don't get to help you pick out a cute outfit or anything, so… that's a bummer."

"One of the drawbacks of being dead, I guess." I shrugged.

"Ooooh, she's going on a date?" Jojo said right beside me, startling Jenny and me with his sudden appearance.

"Jojo, there's a thing called a doorbell," Jenny said, picking up an old soda can from the floor and chucking it at him.

He dodged it lithely. "Yeah, Jenny, I'm not sure if you remember, but ghosts don't need to use the doorbell. It's one of the many reasons being dead is the best."

Jenny rolled her eyes and looked at her phone.

"You're going on a date?" Jojo asked me again. "With *Wuthering Heights* over there?" He paused and scrunched up his face. "I can't remember. What was the name you gave him? It was brilliant." He snapped his fingers as he tried to remember. I honestly couldn't remember, but I let him wrestle with it for a few moments before I jumped in.

"Something about a fancy British something," I said, quite unhelpfully.

"That's it!" Jojo exclaimed, laughing at the memory, even though I hadn't really answered him at all. "Brilliant," he said between laughs.

"First off, it's not a date. I'm showing him around the region so I can keep haunting the Johnstons," I said. "And second, I need to get going. I said I'd meet him in a few minutes."

"It's so sad when our babies grow up," Jojo said, looking over at Jenny, who was still looking down at her phone. "What are you even doing on that thing? Do you really get service in the afterlife? Because I'd like to sign up for that phone plan."

"Can you really get me service?" Jenny asked, her interest finally piqued by something other than her phone.

Jojo thought about this for a moment before frowning. "'Fraid not," he said. "But I'll get in on a selfie any day."

Without waiting for an invitation, Jojo grabbed Jenny's phone and turned it on himself, flashing a peace sign and duck lips. He snapped a quick picture before giving it back to a stunned Jenny.

No one touched her phone. It was common knowledge.

"You're welcome." Jojo grinned. "Have fun on your not-date, kid," he told me before disappearing.

I didn't stick around to see Jenny's reaction to having her phone taken from her in such a brazen manner. Instead, I gave her an apologetic smile and pulled myself from the abandoned house we'd claimed as our own.

There was a moment of weightless confusion before I appeared in front of the darkened front door of the Johnston home. William was waiting for me, looking just as British as ever.

"You're late," he said, his voice monotone.

"Blame Jojo," I answered. "You ready?"

"I've been ready."

"Well, I can already tell this is going to be a super fun evening." I took his hand and disappeared from the Johnston house, only to appear on the boardwalk at Venice beach. I dropped his hand as soon as we arrived.

The sun had turned the sky a brilliant shade of orange, but even with darkness approaching, there were still quite a few people walking in front of the shops.

William looked around the bustling boardwalk, his expression slightly puzzled. "This place is... busy. Do you have much success haunting here?"

I smiled at the familiar boardwalk. "Quiet and solitary aren't always the best circumstances for a haunt," I explained. "This place is great because you can do something super small, so only one person notices, and then no one else will believe them. Because surely, if a ghost had moved something in such a big crowd, more than one person would notice."

"So, you move something in such a way that only one person will really see?" he asked, to which I nodded. "And then you watch as everyone around that person says they're crazy?"

Now I smiled as I nodded.

"That's either brilliant or completely sadistic. I'm not sure which."

"A bit of both, probably." I was dead. There weren't many ways to have fun when you were dead. The way I saw it, I deserved to prank people every once in a while to liven up the afterlife. "Besides, I'm a ghost. That's my job."

"Is it, though?" he asked.

"I mean… the whole point of us is to haunt people. So, yeah, I'd say it's my job."

William furrowed his brow as we walked down the busy boardwalk, avoiding people out of habit, even though they'd walk right through us. "We're not just supposed to haunt people. We're supposed to watch them."

I pulled a face at this. "That sounds a bit creepy."

"Not *watch* them, but watch them," he emphasized, as if this should clear things right up for me. "I've talked to Jojo about it a lot. It doesn't make sense to me that we live a full life, then die only to have our whole purpose be scaring people."

"What did he say?" I asked, my curiosity piqued.

I'd always enjoyed haunting people. It was fun to scare them a little and add some magic into their lives, especially since that "magic" had always been harmless. If anyone ever got too scared, I'd back off. Unless, of course, they seemed like a jerk, in which case I'd double down. But that wasn't really in my job description; it was my vigilante side coming out.

"He said whoever put him in charge of the afterlife was a complete nutter," he said with a laugh.

"Well, that's obvious," I agreed. "I love Jojo, but who in the world thought he was fit to run the entire afterlife?"

"That's the thing," William said, "he doesn't run the entire afterlife."

"Because this is just the first step?" I asked.

I knew not everyone ended up where I was.

"He's not even in charge of the entire first step," William said, surprising me. "There are different… jobs in this first stage of the afterlife."

"Why would Jojo tell you all this but not me?" I asked, slightly offended.

"Did you ask?"

I rolled my eyes. "No, but how am I supposed to know what to ask about? I don't even know what I don't know."

William pressed his lips into a hard line and shrugged, as if this were my fault.

"What else did he say?" I asked, because as annoyed as I was that this was all apparently common knowledge, I wanted to know what these other jobs were.

A group of teenagers whipped by on skateboards too fast for me to move out of the way and passed right through me. It didn't hurt, per se, but it was definitely uncomfortable. I tried to shrug it off, more concerned about what information William had to offer.

"There are Guardians, which, as you can guess, are what the living call guardian angels," he began, looking at the sky as we walked as if he were trying to remember. "Jojo said sometimes Guardians go bad and are then called Beguilers."

"How dramatic," I said. "Is there some sort of afterlife feud we don't even know about?"

"Apparently," he answered. "Our entire department is happy to do what we do and stay out of the drama, I guess."

"It's like all those annoying Backstreet Boys and N*Sync fans," I said, an old annoyance bubbling up after all this time. "And we Hanson fans are just over here, minding our own business, having a good time, and enjoying life."

William ignored my reference. "Well, for whatever reason, our people seem to be relatively unconcerned about such things."

"Maybe that's why we became whatever we are," I mused. "Maybe it has something to do with our personalities?"

"From what I gathered, it's a mix of a lot of things." He looked at me for a brief moment as we walked before turning his eyes forward again. "Personality definitely plays a role. I think there's also how you lived your life. And then unfinished business."

"I knew it!" I shouted, causing William to jump at my unexpected exclamation.

"You have unfinished business?" he asked, raising an eyebrow once he'd gathered himself.

"When my house burned down, I had a VHS of *Poltergeist* inside that I'd rented from Blockbuster," I said, feeling an odd sense of vindication that I'd been right in my "unfinished business" theory. "I never got to return it. And I know that doesn't sound like a big deal, but I'm sort of OCD about these things. 'Be kind, rewind' and all that."

William was giving me a puzzled look. "I understood about half of what you said."

"I know you're from fancy Victorian times, but you've been around since then. You know what a Blockbuster is." He shook his head, his expression blank. "It's this rad place where you go to rent movies," I explained. "It was like, the *best* place to be on a Friday night."

I let a smile grow across my lips as William watched me, moving away momentarily to avoid a couple who were pushing a stroller before falling into step with him.

"Seriously, you haven't lived until you've gone to Blockbuster on a Friday night," I said, reveling in the memories of my past life. "You'd walk in and spend hours browsing the movies. And if it was a really good night, you'd buy candy, popcorn, and soda while you were there." I glanced at William and gave him a grin. "That and watching TGIF on ABC are the things I miss the most about being alive."

William laughed softly at this revelation. "It seems like you can still do some of those things even though you're dead, right?"

I deflated a bit. "I wish. Some dummy decided to get rid

of Blockbuster and put everything on the world wide web instead." I was still bitter about the death of my favorite video rental store. "And TGIF isn't on TV anymore." I frowned. "All good things died with me, I guess. I was just that special."

"I can see that," William joked. "I feel like a lot of your life and afterlife revolve around TV."

I pointed to myself. "90s kid. We were raised by the TV."

"I was raised by a governess," he said. "I guess that's sort of the same thing. Mine just wasn't quite as entertaining as yours."

I nodded, forgetting for a moment we probably had vastly different experiences in life. It wasn't too hard to remember he was from a different time with his fancy gray Victorian suit, but I still didn't know anything about his actual life.

"So, what's your unfinished business?" I asked.

He rubbed the back of his neck, seeming hesitant to tell me.

"Oh, come on," I said. "I told you mine. Fair is fair."

"Fine," he relented, stopping near the short concrete wall that separated the boardwalk from the sandy beach. He looked so out of place there in his nice clothes as a group of surfers walked by without shirts on.

William reached into his jacket pocket and pulled out a dainty gold band. "This is my unfinished business."

I stared at it. "Jewelry design?" I asked, though I knew full well what he was getting at.

He still gave me a courtesy smile for my bad joke, which I appreciated.

"I was going to propose to someone," he said, looking down at the ring. "I thought it would be romantic to take her out in a rowboat on a small lake."

"Did she say no?" I asked, guessing at how this story ended.

"I died," he said simply, putting the ring in his jacket

pocket.

Chapter 6

I raised my eyebrows at the drastic turn the story had taken. How had he gone from proposing to dying? I wanted so desperately to ask, but the frown on his face restrained me. I didn't want to keep digging if the wound was still painful.

Now I felt bad about the whole Blockbuster thing.

"She fell in the water when I moved to get down on one knee," he said. I wasn't sure if he wanted to share his story with me or if he felt rude leaving me hanging. "I jumped in to pull her out since she couldn't swim but didn't realize how shallow the water was."

His lips twitched. "If she would have stood up, she would have been fine. And me, idiot that I was, dove in before she had the chance." He rolled his eyes. "I hit my head on a rock and drowned."

My eyes widened and I tried to refrain from actually letting my mouth fall open. "She couldn't have pulled you out? Worst girlfriend ever."

He gave me a reprimanding look. "She tried, but we wore a lot more clothes back then. And wet clothes are heavy."

"Wasn't the water like… knee deep?" I wasn't buying it. If she was any kind of good fiancée, she would have pulled him out of there somehow.

"It was," he confirmed.

"And yet... you drowned?"

"Isabell loved me," he said firmly. "She didn't let me drown. I'm sure she tried to save me."

"You don't remember?" I asked. Maybe this chick was super nice and actually did try to save him. Maybe she was devastated by her almost-fiancé's death. But it seemed pretty lame that she couldn't have just lifted his head above water and called for help.

"I was knocked out by the rock and I woke up in Jojo's house. I didn't see her attempted rescue, but I know it must have happened."

Ah yes. Jojo's house—the place all of us haunting ghosts woke up. It was so bizarre to be alive one minute and the next a man in a top hat and sneakers grins at you, just waiting to make a bad death pun to soften the blow.

"Sounds suspicious to me." I pressed my lips together.

"Says the girl whose unfinished business is an unreturned VHS tape," he countered.

He had me there. At least his unfinished business was meaningful. Mine was just my OCD coming into play.

That realization made me feel a bit useless.

"So, if we aren't Guardians and we aren't Beguilers, what are we?" I asked, steering the conversation to what William and Jojo had talked about. I didn't want to think about my lackluster unfinished business anymore.

"We're Boons," he said.

"Boons?" I repeated slowly. "What the heck is a Boon?"

"Really?" he asked, his expression unimpressed. "A boon is like... a blessing. Something that's helpful or beneficial in some way."

I mulled this over. It didn't really seem to make sense with how I'd been spending my time.

"Jojo always asks how my haunting is going," I said. "Why would he ask if he knew I was supposed to be doing something helpful? Was I messing up my job this whole time?"

It was bad enough that my unfinished business was so

lame compared to William's, but now I hadn't even been spending the past twenty years doing anything right.

How big of a screw up could I possibly be?

"From what I can tell, you've been doing your job perfectly," he said, in a rare moment of kindness. There wasn't any sarcasm in his voice. "We're here to let people know they aren't alone. For some people, that's the magic of a haunting. Just knowing there's something after death is all they need to keep going."

"Like the Johnstons," I said.

"Like the Johnstons," he agreed. "But we're also here to watch. We watch the people we haunt, and if there's something wrong, we report it to Jojo so he can turn it over to the Guardians."

"Why wouldn't he tell me that?" I asked. "I had no idea that's what I was supposed to be doing."

William had a ghost of a smile on his lips, though I couldn't imagine what he had to smile about right now.

"What?" I asked.

"Maybe he didn't need to tell you," he said. "Have you ever haunted someone who seemed like they may be in trouble? Maybe emotionally?"

I thought about this. "Well… yeah… but I didn't report it to Jojo."

"When he asked you how your hauntings had been going, did you bring it up?"

That sly little Kiwi.

"He's been getting reports out of me without me even knowing it," I said, somewhere between indignation and admiration.

"And that's why he's in charge."

"But he told you about all this?" I asked.

William shrugged. "Some of us aren't instinctually Boons. We need some instruction. He must have known you'd take to it without any prompting. Maybe he thought giving you rules would make the afterlife too boring for you."

"Huh," I said, trying to process everything I'd just learned.

I'd been dead for twenty years, and in the twenty minutes with William, I'd learned everything I'd questioned for so long. I guess I should have asked Jojo if there was more to the afterlife than scaring the pants off of people.

William shifted his weight on the short concrete wall, seeming to grow uncomfortable at my prolonged silence.

"Isn't that your TV beau?" he asked me, nodding toward a surf shop where a small TV outside showed clips from *The Specter Files*.

I immediately forgot about my deep introspection and instead walked through a group of teenagers to get closer to the screen.

It was some sort of Hollywood gossip show, and though I couldn't hear it since the volume was turned off, the headline on the screen was enough to set my heart racing.

Brody Specter was coming to Southern California. He was going to investigate the Grauman's Chinese Theater, which was totally in my district.

I was going to see Brody Specter live and in person.

Or... as "live" as I could be in my current condition.

"What's all this about, then?" William asked.

"I have to get home," I said, my eyes still wide and glued to the screen. "There's so much to do."

Chapter 7

"You're sure we're allowed to be here?" Jenny asked me, looking up from her phone to glance around the darkened theater.

Brody Specter hadn't arrived yet, but the TV crew was already busy setting up cameras around the interior of the Grauman's Chinese Theater. I'd forced Jenny to come with me to meet my crush and may have gotten there much earlier than we needed to. Just in case.

I'd seen the outside of the theater when I'd been alive, but I'd never bothered to go inside. It was beautiful. It made sense since they had so many movie premiers here.

"We're ghosts," I reminded her. "Who's going to stop us?"

"Girl, you know that's not what I meant," she answered, locking eyes with me. "This isn't really one of our haunts. Do you think Jojo is okay with this?"

"I'm sure it's fine." I waved her off, my eyes still scanning the darkened theater. Brody Specter, the beautiful and talented paranormal investigator, would walk through the doors at any moment.

"That wasn't even a little bit reassuring," she said. "This is *so* not in our job description."

I pulled my gaze away from the theater and to my friend. "Dude, did you know we're called Boons?" I asked. "And that we're supposed to watch people to tell Jojo if there are any red flags he needs to pass on to some other department?"

Surely Jenny didn't know all of this. William had probably just bored it out of Jojo.

But when Jenny gave me a look like I was a moron, I got my answer. I didn't need the quick "Uh, duh," that followed the look. But she said it anyway.

"When did you find all that out?" I asked.

"Seriously, Jane?" she asked. "You've been dead *way* longer than me."

"Not *way* longer," I muttered, interrupting her with my indignation.

Even in death, when age wasn't really a thing anymore, I still clung to the habit of being offended by the accusation that I was old.

"Jojo gave me a rundown of the job description right when I woke up in the afterlife. Did you sleep through training or something?"

"He never told me," I practically shouted, feeling the need to defend myself.

Way too many people were questioning my intelligence lately, and I wasn't cool with that.

"Boy toy at twelve o'clock," Jenny said in response to my outburst.

I snapped my head in the direction of the door that led into the theater. We were sitting in the front row of seats near the movie screen so I could make sure I didn't miss Brody.

He'd entered the theater with a camera crew following him around. He spoke to them in that deep, dramatic voice that gave me chills, even though I couldn't hear what he was saying.

"Jenny," I said, tapping her on the shoulder without looking at her. "He's right there."

"Duh, I'm the one who told you that." She sighed.

"No… you don't understand. That's Brody Specter. He's so smart, and beautiful, and perfect, and he's like, twenty feet away."

"Yeah, I got it," she replied, looking down at her phone. "I had way hotter and more famous guys than Brody Specter at my Bat Mitzvah.

How was she so nonchalant when we were in the company of paranormal royalty?

Brody Specter had brown hair that was clipped close to his head, honey eyes, dimples, and a smile that probably would have killed me if I wasn't already dead. I couldn't be sure, since I didn't have a mirror handy, but my eyes had probably been replaced by hearts when I saw him.

"This is pathetic." Jenny sighed beside me. "You look like a lovesick puppy. Go talk to him."

"I'm not allowed to just appear," I said. "This isn't a regular haunt. And I'm trying to keep a low profile so Jojo doesn't catch wind of what I'm doing."

"I knew it," Jenny said, sounding more resigned than mad. "We're going to get into so much trouble."

"I'm just going to pop over to get a closer look," I said with a stupidly happy grin.

I walked toward Brody. He wasn't alone. Two camera men were following him as he held out an EMF reader, talking to the cameras and looking like he did on TV.

"Gosh, you're beautiful," I said as I got closer, the dopey smile still in place.

"The theater is where a few people have reported seeing apparitions," Brody said to the camera, looking intense as he held the EMF meter out.

I approached him slowly.

"I feel a cold spot," Brody said, stopping his forward progression to stand in silence for a moment. "Is there someone here with us?"

I grinned. It was just like the show!

Looking at the device in his hand, I wondered if I was really bold enough to try to touch it. Just being here with Brody was dangerous enough, but trying to make contact with him felt like being actively disobedient.

Steeling myself, I reached out and touched the EMF meter, watching as the rainbow of lights ignited across its surface, the device emitting a high-pitched beep.

This was so incredible. I got to be a part of my favorite show! I couldn't wait until the episode aired, so I could tell the Johnstons it was me they were hearing. I mean… they wouldn't be able to hear me talking to them, but it was the principle of the thing.

"Did you get that?" Brody asked the camera man beside him, who nodded. "There's definitely something here."

It was me. I was the "something" who was there. Brody Specter was talking about me!

Brody put the EMF meter away in his pocket and pulled out a spirit box. Personally, I always hated when those ghost hunting shows used spirit boxes; none of the ghosts I knew actually communicated through them. It was just living humans hearing what they wanted in the random mess of radio noise.

But could *I* use it to communicate?

Touching an EMF meter and manipulating a radio signal to talk to Brody were two very different things. I wasn't even sure how it would work.

"We're going to do a spirit box session to see if we can make contact with the entity," Brody said to the camera. It was so surreal to see him in person when I'd watched him do this exact thing every Wednesday. "Did you die here?" Brody asked, closing his eyes to listen intently to the device that was quickly flipping through stations of radio static. His lashes were so thick that when his eyes were closed, they brushed against his cheeks.

Focus, Jane.

"No," I said, placing my hand on the spirit box.

It took a few moments, but after flipping through a few radio stations, clear as day, a male voice said "no" through the spirit box.

Brody and I both jumped in unison.

"It worked," I said, shouting at Jenny, who was probably still glued to her phone.

Brody stared at the device, a small smile beginning to play on his lips.

We were talking. I was talking to Brody Specter. This was incredible. I'd never talked to a living person before. At least not since I'd died.

"Okay, so this presence didn't die here," he said, turning to the cameras for a moment as he explained this before turning back to his spirit box. "What's your name?"

Having a spirit box say "no" hadn't been too hard. But saying my name was incredibly specific. Would I be able to do it?

I touched the device once more and concentrated, not that I knew if it would help or not. But I figured it couldn't hurt. "Jane."

Brody and I both stared at the spirit box, waiting to hear a name come through the static. I took my hand off of the device, wondering if that would speed up the process.

One moment passed. And then another. It was only seconds but felt like an eternity before a muffled voice said, "Jen."

"Jenny!" I yelled, "I'm sort of doing it!"

She didn't respond.

"Jen," Brody exclaimed, looking at the cameras again, his honey-colored eyes wide with wonder.

Brody Specter had said my name... almost. It was close enough. My fangirl heart gave a leap.

"What exactly do you two think you're doing here?" Jojo said from the front of the theater where Jenny was standing.

"It was Jane's idea," Jenny said, automatically ratting me out.

That butthead.

I turned around to meet Jojo's eyes, looking so incredibly guilty. Panic rose inside of me as I realized Jojo would soon pull us away from this location. What I was doing was too public. People couldn't have such solid proof of the afterlife. But I couldn't let this be the only time I ever saw Brody face to face. I had to do something quickly.

Placing my hand back on the spirit box, I concentrated as

hard as I could and said, "California. Ramona. Abandoned house."

I felt Jojo's hand on my shoulder and was pulled from the theater before I could tell if my words had come through the other end of the spirit box.

Had it worked?

Or had I just broken so many rules for nothing?

Either way, the look of annoyance on Jojo's face when we arrived in Ramona suggested it didn't matter. I was in serious trouble.

Chapter 8

Jojo and I stared at each other in silence.

Jenny wasn't with us, but I figured Jojo had decided to let her off the hook, since this whole thing had obviously been my idea.

I stared at him and he stared at me, and we stayed like that for a long time. I didn't want to be the first one to talk, but the silence was becoming unbearable.

Right when I thought I'd crack and say something, Jojo spoke. "Do you think I'm pulling this jacket off?"

He wore a white jacket with pictures of traffic signs all over it. It was loud and odd, and I couldn't quite place what time period it belonged to.

I didn't really think he was pulling it off, but I didn't want to push my luck. Technically, I had broken a few rules, and the last thing I needed was Jojo in a bad mood when I was already on thin ice.

"You look flawless."

He narrowed his eyes. "Good answer," he said, accepting the lie. "Now, onto the second order of business: you trying to expose the entirety of the afterlife because you have a crush on a pseudo-celebrity."

I inhaled sharply. Brody Specter was *not* a pseudo-celebrity. He was a legitimate ghost hunter and paranormal researcher.

His status as a connoisseur of the paranormal wasn't diminished just because he happened to have a TV show. It proved he wanted to share his gift with the world.

If anything, Jojo should have appreciated his work.

Of course, I didn't say any of that. "Sorry."

I was pretty sure Jojo didn't know I'd tried to tell Brody where to find me. If my message never went through the spirit box, I wouldn't have to explain myself. If it did... I'd have to have another uncomfortable talk with Jojo.

Better to ask forgiveness than ask permission, I guess.

"I give you a *lot* of slack, and you keep pushing your limits. It's like you want me to banish you to Hell or something."

My eyes widened. "You can do that?"

Jojo laughed. "Of course not." He paused, furrowing his brow. "I don't think. I haven't really tried it before." Jojo looked like he'd just had a revelation. "I should try it out on Nick from the PR department. Just to see if I can."

"Please don't," I said, figuring that Nick wouldn't be too happy about being accidentally banished to Hell.

"We'll work out the details later," he said with a wave. "Back to serious matters."

"More serious than banishing someone to Hell?"

Jojo leveled his eyes. "Yes." He wasn't normally very intimidating, but this look actually made me nervous. "I know you think Brody Specter is dreamy AF... that's a 1990s thing, right?"

"AF?" I asked. "Sounds more like Jenny's time."

"The point is, you can't let a cute boy make you expose the entirety of the afterlife. That's not fair to the rest of us who are just going about our business, being good little ghosts."

"I really am sorry." I meant it. But I didn't bother mentioning the fact that if I had the chance to do it again, I'd definitely take it. "But that being said, aren't you in charge of like... all the ghosts? How do you have so much time to keep an eye on me?"

"Because, dear Jane, none of my other ghosts give me quite

so much trouble. You're the only one who requires constant attention."

I winced. I was pretty sure he wasn't being facetious. I did sort of mess up a lot.

"That actually reminds me, I'm mad at you," I said, pointing an accusing finger at Jojo.

He looked taken aback. "Wait... you're mad at me?" he said, trying to wrap his head around this new information. "But... but I'm mad at you right now. You being mad at me throws me off my game."

Hopefully it would throw him off his game enough for him to forget I broke some big rules. "You never told me anything about the afterlife. Or about Boons. You never told me anything about anything," I said. "You cut me loose to figure it out as I went. And you let me believe we're supposed to haunt people. Do you know how embarrassing that is when I run into another ghost?"

Jojo laughed. "Oh yeah, that part was sort of intentional. But technically haunting is part of your job description. It's not your entire job, like I may have let you believe. Or... it sort of is your entire job... it's just not the purpose of the job to scare people."

"I had to have William, the fancy British boy, tell me about the job I've been doing for twenty years." I put my hands over my face. "That was a fun conversation."

"Oh, I so wish I'd been there for it," Jojo said with a fond smile. "I need some cheering up every now and then. I'm not always rainbows and sunshine, you know? I'm still a person."

He was changing the subject, but I wasn't having it. "So, why didn't you tell me?"

Jojo paused, as if he hadn't been in this conversation with me the whole time. "Tell you what?"

"Jojo!" I exclaimed. "About my purpose in the afterlife! How could you not tell me any of it?"

Jojo shrugged, causing the gaudy white jacket with traffic signs on it to slouch off a bit. "You were already such a natural. I didn't need to tell you what to do. You figured it out on your own."

"Don't you think I could have been a bit more efficient if you'd let me know what my job actually was?"

"Huh," he said simply, as if the thought had never occurred to him.

I was dealing with a child.

A 500-year-old man-child.

"Well?" he asked.

"Well, what?"

"What do you want to know?"

I raised my eyebrows. "Um… everything?"

"That's a lot, but okay. In the beginning—"

"Jojo, I'm serious," I said. "At the very least, I need to know what my job description is."

"I know that one," he said, as if he were a kid in school who had just been called on by the teacher. "Boon."

"Which is?"

"You watch people and let them know they aren't alone. And… you know… other serious stuff. Like if they seem like they're in trouble, then you report to me and blah, blah, blah."

"No 'blah, blah, blah'," I said. "That's the stuff I need to know. You keep skipping over the essential parts."

Jojo sighed while rolling his eyes, which was an impressive feat. It was more exasperation than I'd ever managed to fit into one expression in my living teenage years.

"Haunting people gives them some clue there's something after life. And hauntings are something that can't be explained away by science so… it's an effective and easy way to make people feel like they aren't alone," Jojo said. "The unexplainable proof of the afterlife transcends science, religion, philosophy… all of it. That's why we haunt."

"You couldn't have said exactly that when I showed up at your place after dying?" I asked.

"You were so bent out of shape over the fact that you didn't return *Poltergeist* to Blockbuster, I barely had time to tell you about regions and haunting in general."

That was fair.

Sort of.

Jojo took a deep, long-suffering breath before saying, "Here," and pulling a huge scroll from behind his back to hand to me.

When he handed it over, I dropped the scroll, letting it unravel as it rolled across the living room floor. It stretched on for several feet and hadn't even begun unraveling all the way.

"That's... a lot of rules," I said, suddenly wondering if I really wanted all of this information.

"I can make it a bit more accessible to what you're comfortable with," Jojo said, snapping his fingers so the scroll disappeared. Suddenly, he was holding a colorful copy of a magazine that looked suspiciously like *Tiger Beat*. Only this magazine had a picture of Jojo on the front, smiling widely while giving the camera a thumbs up. Under his picture there was a caption that read, "Everything you ever wanted to know about the afterlife but were too afraid to ask."

I gave him a skeptical look as I took the magazine, scanning the cover again to see there was a second headline that read, "This century's hottest fashion for that perfect undead summer."

"I don't know if I'm insulted you gave me the rules in the form of a magazine or grateful," I said.

"There's also a poster of me you can pull out and hang on your wall," he added, seeming particularly proud of this detail.

"I'll get right on that." I set the magazine down and wondered who would have possibly put Jojo in charge of any department of the afterlife.

"All right, kiddo. This was fun," he said, giving me a quick wink. "So, no more Graumen's Chinese Theater for you, right?"

"Technically, the Graumen's Chinese Theater is in haunting public domain," I mumbled.

"I guess I should rephrase," he said. "No more trying to expose the afterlife to every warm blood with internet access, all right?"

I gave him a small salute. Both because it was a gesture I knew would end the conversation, and because I knew it was just vague enough for me to get away with seeing Brody again.

"That's a good ghost," he said. "Have fun with my poster. It's dreamy AF."

"Still not talking to someone from the right time period for that," I said, just as Jojo disappeared from the house.

Chapter 9

"Did you know you're allowed to make cold spots appear, but not hot spots?" I asked Jenny as we sat on the roof of the abandoned house in Ramona. I was lazily flipping through the *Tiger Beat* afterlife rule book Jojo had given me.

Jenny was lying on her back with her eyes closed, letting the setting sun wash over her in a vain attempt to get a tan. I suspected it was an old habit from her living days, but didn't want to ruin her fun.

"Yeah, the afterlife is all about making stuff cold for some reason," she answered, keeping her eyes closed as she spoke.

"Weird," I said in a distracted way before continuing. "Also, you're allowed to open cupboards and doors, but you can't open a refrigerator."

"Girl, how do you seriously not know any of this?" Jenny asked.

She propped herself up on her elbows and glanced over at the magazine I was holding.

"Oh. Em. Gee. I love *Tiger Beat*!" she squealed, grabbing it out of my hands to scan the glossy pages.

"Was *Tiger Beat* still around when you were alive?" I asked, figuring it would have gone the way of Blockbuster and A.O.L. Instant Messenger.

"I'm pretty sure it's *still* a thing," she said before sitting up all the way to nudge me with her elbow. "Is it just me, or does Jojo look fine in these pictures?"

I looked over at the page she was studying. It was the one that talked about how a Boon could write in the steam on a mirror, but only if they didn't write an entire word. For some reason, Jojo had thought it was necessary to wear a towel wrapped around his chest like a girl with another towel turban on his head. He pouted at the camera, giving a thumbs down to indicate the example in the picture, which spelled out "murder" was unacceptable.

"What is with these pictures?" I asked, squinting at the absurdity before me.

"I don't know," Jenny said, still staring at it. "He's got a little something going on. His face is sort of gorgeous."

"Jenny, he's like... more than 500 years older than you."

"Don't be like that. Age isn't a thing after you die," she said, waving away my concerns while flipping through a few more pages of the magazine.

As the sun dipped behind the distant mountains, it was getting harder to see the pictures. It also made it hard to see the figure who was suddenly standing on the other side of the roof across from us.

"Jane?" William called, causing me to jump.

I seemed to do that a lot around him.

"You scared me to death," I said, placing my hand over my rapidly beating heart that was completely useless in the afterlife. Who needed a heartbeat when they were a ghost?

There were a lot of weirdly arbitrary things like that in the afterlife.

"Already dead," Jenny said, looking up from the magazine to give William the once over. She raised her eyebrows, then looked over at me with a smirk.

"I apologize for showing up unannounced," William said, approaching slowly. "I don't make social calls often and... I wasn't sure how to properly announce myself when I found you weren't inside of the house."

"Yeah, there's not really a doorbell for the roof." I smiled. "Sorry about that. We like to watch the sunset up here."

Jenny tossed the *Tiger Beat* magazine at me and stood up, dusting off her bum as she did so. "I'm Jenny, by the way," she said, holding her hand out and smiling at William.

He took her hand and gave a small nod. "William."

"You must be the new guy in town," she said. "Jane told me all about your little arrangement, but she failed to give me the more important details." At this statement, Jenny looked over at me and raised her eyebrows suggestively.

"Okay," I interjected, standing up quickly and grabbing William's hand away from Jenny's. "Did you want me to show you around some more?"

I hoped if I talked quickly enough, I could stop Jenny from saying anything too embarrassing.

"You know what? I'll take you to another one of my favorite spots. Bye, Jenny," I said hurriedly. And with that, I pulled us away from Jenny and the house and onto the deck of a large ship.

William looked a bit flustered as we reappeared. "That was... abrupt."

I winced, knowing that was a bit rude. Ghosts usually warned each other before just changing locations. "Sorry about that. Jenny can be... a bit much."

"I was starting to get that feeling," he answered, laughing softly.

When he smiled, little lines appeared on his cheeks. Prominent dimples. I hadn't noticed them until now.

It made me smile involuntarily.

"So, where are we now?" he asked, looking around the deck.

The three large red steam stacks on the ship had a string of white lights strung above them. The lights were attached to the mast, then strung down to where we stood, illuminating the deck in the dark, warm, southern California night.

"This is one of the best places to haunt," I said with a grin. "It's public domain, so anyone can haunt. And it's constantly full of people looking for ghosts."

William turned to get a better look at the ship, and the movement made me realize I was still holding his hand from when I'd brought us here.

I couldn't remember the last time I'd held someone's hand. It had to be before I'd died. It felt... nice to touch someone again. It wasn't like I had a lot of physical contact in my haunts. I didn't think living people could actually feel me if I touched them, anyway. But ghosts were as physical for each other as two living people were. We were just a solitary lot by nature.

But here I was. Holding William's hand. Touching someone deliberately for the first time in twenty years.

I sort of liked it.

My cheeks flushed, but I didn't want to suddenly pull away from him. That would only draw attention to the fact that I'd been holding his hand in the first place.

Instead, I began walking toward the interior of the ship and let my hand fall from his as I approached the door. That seemed natural, right?

"Let's see if we can find any people looking for a scare," I said, my voice sounding funny.

I glanced over my shoulder at William, who was watching me walk away. He seemed to realize he was staring and looked a bit guilty before joining me by the door. "It's the middle of the week. Do you really think we'll find fans of the paranormal here right now?"

We began walking through the long hallways of the ship's interior. "I failed to mention this isn't just any ship. This is The Queen Mary. It's known to be haunted, and they turned it into a hotel with ghost tours and stuff. People come here *because* it's haunted. It doesn't matter what day of the week it is."

William followed beside me, his head turning from side to side as if he were looking for something. "There *is* a strange feeling on this ship," he said. "Like... a presence. But it's not us."

"There are other ghosts on this ship besides us," I told him.

"I can tell. Feels like some Guardians," he drawled, his voice distant, as if he were concentrating on what he could feel. "And maybe... a Kin?"

"What's a Kin?" I asked, glancing over as we continued walking through the hallways.

"It's exactly what it sounds like. It's a person who has passed on but needs to give a message to a living relative. But there's something else I can't quite place." William frowned at this. "Something not quite... ghosty."

I laughed at his word choice. "Ghosty? That word seems so funny coming from someone so—" I gestured to him.

He gave me a sideways smile but continued. "I'm not sure how else to put it. It's something paranormal, but not a person who was once alive. It's like... a creature."

"How can you sense all of this?" I asked. "All I know is this place feels like it's haunted... but not by us."

"The longer you're dead, the easier it is to pick up on this kind of thing," he said. "Plus, England is older. It has a lot more ghosts and creatures than the United States, so I've been exposed to more than you probably have."

I nodded but felt a bit out of the loop once more. This proved I didn't know enough about the afterlife to have any sense of how ignorant I was. Until a few days ago, I hadn't known there were different types of ghosts, let alone creatures who didn't actually fall into the category of "ghost."

"So, there are non-human things in this world other than ghosts?" I asked as we stopped our trek in front of a random door I could sense some people behind.

"Where do you think all the folklore comes from?" he asked.

I smiled. This was getting interesting. "What kind of creatures are there?"

"Basically, anything you've heard about in a scary story originated with some small bit of truth," he said, glancing at my smile and matching it with his own. I was hanging on his every word. "Sirens, poltergeists, doppelgangers... you name it, it exists."

"This. Is. Awesome." I emphasized every word with a pause, beaming.

Eternity just got a lot more interesting.

"Have you seen any of these creatures?" I asked, stepping closer.

He swallowed before answering. "We usually can't see them. We can only see other types of ghosts."

"Well, that's a bummer," I said.

William seemed to sense my disappointment and quickly spoke up. "But it's not totally impossible to see them. They can show themselves to us just like we can show ourselves to living humans sometimes."

"We'll have to experiment with that soon," I said, smiling once more.

William returned the smile again, shifting ever-so-slightly closer to me. It immediately showed me just how close we'd gotten.

"There are definitely some people in this room." I took a step back, changing the subject as smoothly as I could. "We should try to give them a scare."

"That *is* why we came," he agreed, his smile seeming less genuine all of a sudden.

I didn't like it. I missed his dimples already, even though I'd only noticed them a few minutes ago.

"Let's see who we've got in here," I said, walking into the dimly lit cabin.

Two tall men sat at a table in the small room. Though they couldn't look more opposite from each other if they tried, I knew they were related. I'd seen them before.

One was pale with straight blond hair, blue eyes, and glasses, while the other had dark olive skin, curly brown hair, and green eyes.

"So… you and Sadie show up at my room in the middle of the night wearing your pajamas, and I'm not supposed to ask about that?" the blond one asked.

The brunette smiled. "What exactly would you like to know,

cousin?"

"They're British," William exclaimed with a smile.

"Is it making you homesick?" I joked.

"A bit, actually."

Oops. Smooth move, Jane.

"You know exactly what I'd like to know," the blond said, raising his eyebrows.

The dark-haired man tilted his head to the side, still smiling, as if he was enjoying watching the other man beat around the bush. "Sadie thought she had a paranormal encounter and was seeking my expertise."

"Looks like someone beat us to the haunting," William said, disappointment lining his voice.

"I want to believe you're lying to me, and the story is actually better than that, but something tells me it's not," the blond said.

"We can't haunt them, anyway," I told William. "I've seen these guys before. They're part of a paranormal investigation team. Jojo got kind of mad at me for making contact with a paranormal investigator a few days ago."

William watched me, his eyes searching my expression. I was guessing the emotions he'd find would be embarrassment, disappointment, and a bit of frustration. "Haunting paranormal investigators is generally frowned upon," he agreed, pausing to give me a devilish smile before continuing. "But it's not totally against the rules." His deep voice seemed to get even deeper as he spoke.

Why was that so attractive?

"Are you actually suggesting we bend the rules?" I asked, finding it hard to believe that law-abiding William would ever willingly go against Jojo's wishes.

He leaned in closer to me, still smiling and making my useless pulse pick up a few ticks. "What's an afterlife without a little risk?"

Chapter 10

We waited for the two men to fall asleep before we made our move. I sat on the floor next to the bed so that I was eye-level with the brunette as he slept. William sat beside me, our legs touching.

It was probably going to take a long time for me to get used to the feeling of physically touching another person again. Jenny and I were friends, but we weren't exactly cuddling and braiding each other's hair every night. I didn't realize how touch-starved I'd been all these years.

"What do you think we should do?" I asked.

"You choose," he told me.

We were sitting so close together. I wasn't sure if it was Jenny's not-so-subtle hint at how attractive William was or my own encounter with Brody Specter that had reminded me what a crush felt like, but I was suddenly noticing a lot more about William.

His shaggy black hair. His dimples when he smiled. His excellent jawline.

There was a lot more there to admire than I'd realized. It was becoming distracting.

"Well, they have a camera set up in the corner of the room," I pointed out. "I think they're hoping to catch a voice or something on the audio. Maybe you should go whisper something?"

Was this an excuse for me to get some distance between us? I needed to focus, and having him right next to me wasn't doing the trick.

William walked over to the camera, leaning in close. "In case anyone is wondering what a terrifying ghostly apparition looks like, I'll describe it to you in great detail." He grinned now as he continued to talk into the camera. "It's got blonde hair and a black velvet choker that was sort of a trend back in my day and apparently made a reappearance later in life. It wears this black dress with sunflowers on it, which hints at femininity, but then throws you off with black combat boots. It's sort of intimidating and uses ridiculous slang that probably wasn't even popular when it was alive. But it's also very passionate about understanding everything around it."

William raised his eyebrows. "Did I miss anything?"

"You didn't mention my killer smiley face ring," I said, holding up my hand. "This thing is a choice."

"She also wants me to tell you she has a, and I quote, 'killer smiley face ring'." He nodded as if he'd done his job before pausing. "She also has the warmest smile I've ever seen."

Seriously? Why did he have to go and say that? And right before he came back to sit on the ground with me?

I inhaled and held my breath, not sure what I should say to that. It would probably be best to brush it off as a joke. Or maybe I should make a snarky comment. But I sort of loved what he'd said about my smile.

And I loved that he'd noticed.

"Well done, sir," I said, trying to sound very business-like as I patted him on the back.

Who patted someone on the back? That was such a dumb move.

"Hopefully their camera picked up at least some of that." He rested against the wall, his shoulder touching mine.

"From my experience messing with paranormal investigators, they'll probably just hear a sigh or something," I said. "But I appreciate the enthusiasm for our haunt."

"I suppose we could always make the light flicker or turn the tap on or something," William suggested, before looking over my shoulder and turning as white as—well—a ghost.

Was that an offensive saying to the dead?

"I've always been partial to stealing a single sock," Jojo said, suddenly sitting on the other side of me so I was wedged in between him and William. "I know it's juvenile, but there's something so classically frustrating about stealing one sock. Plus, it's our duty to perpetuate the rumors about where all of those socks go."

Jojo must have seen the way the color drained from my face as well, because he gave me a wide smile as he chewed on some gum. He loved it when he caught me off guard. I secretly suspected he kept close tabs on me just so he could find out when I was making a mistake and pop up to scare me.

"Jojo," William said, sounding shocked. "This was my fault. Jane was just showing me around the region to help familiarize me with Southern California. She brought me to this ship and when we found these gentlemen, she said we couldn't haunt them."

"They're paranormal investigators," I mumbled.

"Exactly. Which is what she said to me when we saw them," William went on, sort of word vomiting. "But I wanted to seem daring in front of her and suggested we haunt them, anyway. So, this is completely my fault."

Jojo watched the two of us stammering over our words with mild amusement, nodding as we spoke. Once we both fell silent, he smiled again. "Oh, no sweat, mate," he said with a wave of his hand.

I narrowed my eyes at this casual dismissal of something that was apparently a big deal. "Wait... seriously? I talk to Brody Specter, and you go all 'let's send someone to Hell', but when William purposefully breaks the rules, it's all bros before—"

"First off," Jojo interrupted. "You'll find I don't use that word, Jane. I'm a gentleman." As if to emphasize his point, Jojo smoothed his curly salt and pepper hair. "And second, it's not okay because *William* did it. It's okay because I ship you guys. So, I'm all for this cute little back-and-forth thing you've got going on."

My eyes widened. Had he really just said that right in front of William?

"You ship us?" William asked, completely confused as he looked around the ship we were currently on. Apparently, he didn't know what shipping was. And that might have just saved me from an afterlife of humiliation. If I played my cards right, I could convince him it had something to do with maritime trivia.

"Not sure what your ship name would be," Jojo went on. I had to stop this. "Maybe like... Jilliam? Or... Wane?" Jojo paused and adopted a confused look. "No wait... that's a real name... that wouldn't work."

"What on earth are you talking about?" William asked.

"He's just being Jojo." I placed my hand over Jojo's mouth to stop him from explaining what "shipping" was. The second I felt a wet sensation against my skin, I pulled my hand away in disgust. "Did you just lick me?" I asked, wiping my hand on Jojo's yellow pineapple shirt.

"It's very rude to put your hand over someone's mouth," he stated matter-of-factly. "Hopefully you've learned your lesson, young lady."

"Definitely," I said. "And we're sorry about breaking the rules again. We'll just get going."

"I'd greatly appreciate that," the dark-haired man in the bed said. "Because even if I came here to find ghosts, I also came here to find sleep. And you lot are being incredibly loud right now."

William and I froze, but Jojo just laughed. "Jojo can... can he hear us?" I asked, keeping my eyes trained on the man in front of us.

He opened his large green eyes and looked right at me, adopting an expression of annoyance. "I can see you, too," he said in a deep monotone.

I glanced at William, who looked just as shocked as I felt. He stared, open-mouthed, at the man without saying anything. It looked like he'd seen a ghost, even though the opposite was true.

"How have you been, Jefferson?" Jojo asked. "Still chasing the dream?"

"Clearly," the man said, his lips tugging in a slight smile. "How's the afterlife, Jojo? Still in charge of everything, or have you accidentally burned the place down yet?"

"Oh, trust me, when I burn it down, it won't be an accident," Jojo said, sounding like he was joking with an old friend rather than speaking to a living human. Totally against the rules.

The fact that he'd just yelled at me the day before for doing this very thing only brought up a mild sense of indignation. I was too busy staring at the living human man who was talking to three ghosts like it was no big deal.

"Sorry about these two," Jojo said, nodding over toward William and me. "So rude."

"No problem," Jefferson responded. "I know you have your hands full with green ghosts." At his words, his cousin stirred, talking in his sleep before the brunette, Jefferson, nudged him with his elbow. "Go back to sleep, Deacon. You're dreaming." He smiled at Jojo. "He still isn't ready to handle this whole situation."

"Best to keep them in the dark sometimes," Jojo agreed.

"You're good at doing that," I mumbled, forgetting for a moment how weird it was to be talking to a living person.

"Excuse me, young lady?" Jojo said. "I think my *Tiger Beat* magazine pretty well covered the rules of the afterlife."

"Am I missing something here?" William asked. "Because I'm a bit confused."

"Jojo, you know I always love a visit from you," Jefferson said. "But I have a long day ahead of me, and I've already been woken up once because of a paranormal encounter. Do you think you three can discuss this in the hallway?"

"Of course! So sorry for the intrusion. You, sir," he said,

pointing at Jefferson, "are a gentleman and a scholar. You keep up the good work."

"It was good to see you, Jojo," Jefferson said, giving William and me a curt nod before turning over in bed.

"You two, march," Jojo instructed, ushering us into the hallway. "You totally embarrassed me in front of Jefferson back there. Not cool, guys."

"Okay, what in the actual heck is going on here, Jojo?" I had a million questions, but the most important one was obvious. "How could that guy see and hear us?"

"Yes, I'd like to know that as well," William agreed. "That whole exchange was rather odd."

"Understood," Jojo said. "It's not that complicated. Some people are special and are closer to our plane than others. Easy peasy."

"Not easy peasy," I said, pointing an accusing finger at Jojo. "Is this another one of those things I should know but you just never bothered to tell me? Like the fact that there are other creatures besides ghosts?"

"Clearly you don't need me to tell you if you already know," he said, shrugging.

"I only know because William told me."

At the mention of William, Jojo got a big grin on his face, looking between the two of us.

Oh no.

"Oh yeah. Dear William," Jojo said, his voice sly. "On the topic of things we don't understand, I'm going to leave you to explain to William what 'shipping' is. Have fun!"

And with that, he was gone.

I stared at the empty space in the hallway where Jojo once stood, not wanting to turn around and look at William. Was I clever enough to make up a lie on the fly? Probably not.

"Is this a term everyone but me knows?" William asked, prompting me to turn around and face him. He looked adorably confused. "I may be from a different time, but I've been around since then. I usually pick up on colloquialisms."

"The fact that you just said 'colloquialisms' tells me maybe you don't pick up on them as much as you think you do."

"I suppose that's a fair point." He rubbed the back of his neck. "But I get the feeling you don't want to tell me what shipping means. Is it rude?"

"Not exactly." How long could I draw this out? I could always take the coward's way out and just disappear.

William pursed his lips. "Enlighten me."

I sighed. "Fine." I leaned against the wall and crossed my arms over my chest. William joined me. "A 'ship' is like a relationship. So, when you 'ship' two people, it means you want them to be together in some romantic capacity. Usually it's reserved for talking about fictional characters, but apparently, Jojo thinks of us as fictional characters."

I said all of this quickly so I wouldn't chicken out. After a moment, I ventured a glance at William, who was now puckering his lips to one side and nodding silently.

"I mean… we are pretty adorable," William said. "You can't blame him for recognizing that."

I nodded but didn't say anything. I had only started realizing William was more than an annoyance to my afterlife. I wasn't ready to admit anything.

Seeming to sense I didn't want to comment on the situation, he spoke, putting me out of my misery. "It's pretty late, and I've still got a few families to check in on. Is it okay if I call on you in a few days to show me around a bit more?"

Thank goodness he was such a gentleman. He wasn't pressing me on the issue.

I smiled, letting the warmth of it fill my cheeks. "Of course."

He smiled back easily, making his dimples stand out. His smile was devastating. "I'll see you then."

Chapter 11

I spent the next night haunting a few of my regulars, checking in on them while flickering a few lights. Now that I knew I was supposed to actually be watching out for any warning signs that these people might be in trouble, my job seemed a bit more difficult.

But then again, according to what I'd read in Jojo's *Tiger Beat* magazine, Guardians were the ghosts who were actually supposed to watch out for the wellbeing of living humans. Boons were there to make them feel "not so alone." And if we happened to notice something the Guardians had missed, we reported it to Jojo.

That last part was throwing me off. What if I wasn't watching these households closely enough?

I mulled this over in the darkened living room of our abandoned home in Ramona. With Jenny out haunting, I had some alone time. At least, I assumed she was haunting. Knowing her she was spying on celebrities or going on some kind of ghost date. Even in the afterlife, her social life was full.

"Is there anyone here?" I heard a familiar voice say.

At first, I thought maybe Jojo had blessed us with a TV. But it wasn't Wednesday... so Brody Specter wouldn't be on TV right now, anyway.

That could only mean...

"Brody..." I said, my eyes wide as I turned to see him standing in the doorway of the abandoned house. *My* abandoned house. "I can't believe you came!"

Of course, he couldn't hear me, but it still felt nice to pretend to talk to him.

It was sort of amazing he'd found my house. I wasn't sure he'd gotten my message through the spirit box before Jojo had pulled me away. But here he was. In the flesh. Brody Specter.

I refrained from squealing like a fangirl, even though I wanted to.

"I'm going to place this spirit book on the floor," Brody said, completely unaware of my presence. "If you want to write me a message, it's right here for you."

He placed a pen and a book with blank pages on the ground and stepped away from it slowly, watching it as he did so. He was so cute. And obviously nervous, which made me smile.

I walked to the spirit book and scrunched up my face at it, narrowing my eyes. What made this a "spirit book" and not just some random journal? Was it imbued with paranormal energy or something? I'd never used one before, but I wasn't even sure if they were one of the approved methods of communication. I'd skipped over that page in the rule book.

"I already know contacting Brody is against the rules, so does it really matter what the method is?" I asked no one in particular.

Jojo hadn't shown up, which meant he must not know what was going on. Normally, if he knew I was up to something, he'd pop up right away. Maybe he was distracted.

A gnawing worry grew annoyingly in my gut, but I tried to ignore it. "Better to ask forgiveness than ask permission, right?"

With this poor excuse for justification, I knelt down and picked up the pen. The pen itself didn't actually move in the real world, but I could still feel it between my fingers, even without seeing it there. It was spooky. I knew that as spirits, we existed on our own plane and could interact with the physical world in a roundabout way, but that didn't make this any less foreign to me.

I pressed on the page where I estimated the tip of the pen would have been, and as I did so, a dot of ink appeared in the book.

"This is so cool," I breathed.

Brody had left the room and was placing other equipment into the bedrooms of the house, so I had some time to figure this spirit book out before he returned.

I tried to draw a line on the page, but it was shaky and uneven at best. This was harder than it looked. That meant I had to be short and to the point with my message.

No cameras.

I hoped that was good enough. At least if he listened to that message, I could try to appear to him.

Jojo's big issue with me contacting Brody seemed to be that he had a TV show. As Boons, we were supposed to let people know there's something after death. We couldn't just go around dropping definitive evidence for the entire world all at once. There had to be a personal aspect to it. And that was harder and harder now that AOL and SixDegrees had turned into every kind of social media platform you could imagine.

If I could get Brody to agree to talk to me without documenting any of it, I couldn't see why Jojo would have a problem. It was just one person. One person who would hopefully swear he wouldn't talk about this encounter on his TV show.

Maybe this plan wasn't as well thought out as I'd hoped. How could I expect the host of a paranormal TV show to talk to a full-bodied apparition without mentioning it on his show?

"No cameras," Brody said right beside me, startling me.

Apparently, William wasn't the only one who could sneak up on me.

I turned to look at Brody, only to realize we were standing incredibly close. This intimate proximity made my breath catch in my chest, but I had to remind myself that since he couldn't see me, it didn't really count.

"You're even beautiful up close," I said, not even a little ashamed of how swoony I was being. No one was there to see it.

"I won't turn on any cameras," Brody said, his voice too loud for how close we were.

I took a step back, just in case he decided to shout again.

"I'm going to sit next to this spirit book and ask you some questions. I won't use a camera or recording device, so I'll need you to speak up or else I won't be able to hear you," he said.

"Yeah, you won't be able to hear me anyway," I answered, waiting for him to sit on the ground before I took a seat directly across from him.

The spirit book sat in between us, but I didn't know how well I'd be able to use it.

"Is this the same spirit I spoke to at the Graumen's Chinese Theater?" Brody asked, his voice still too loud. It made me smile.

"Okay, Jane. This is it," I said to myself. "No going back. I've already contacted him, so it's not like I can get into *more* trouble."

I closed my eyes and concentrated. I could feel my body getting warmer, like when your blood rushes back to your foot after it's fallen asleep. The sensation spread through my entire body, and I evened out my breathing.

I'd never been very good at appearing to people. Mostly because I'd never had any reason to do it. The moody 90s kid aesthetic didn't exactly scream, "terror."

"Out of practice," I said when I realized I still hadn't appeared.

I gave myself a little shake and closed my eyes again, concentrating as hard as I could.

How would I even know if I'd appeared?

"I—" Brody began, though he didn't finish his sentence.

I opened my eyes, and he was staring right at me with his mouth open so wide I thought his jaw might fall off.

"Can you see me?" I asked, feeling like the shock on my face might rival his own.

Brody nodded slowly, his mouth hanging open. He still couldn't speak, which made me feel pretty impressive. How many paranormal encounters had he had before? He shouldn't have been *this* impressed by me.

"Sorry to just… appear. I wasn't even sure I could do it. I didn't mean to scare you," I said, now feeling a little awkward. I didn't really think this would work. Now that it had, I didn't know what to do next.

Brody continued to stare. He'd slowly closed his mouth, so that was an improvement, though his eyes were still huge.

"So… I'm Jane," I said, my voice now tight from how painfully awkward this was becoming. "I'm… dead."

Seriously? This was how I made small talk with my celebrity crush?

"Um… I'm glad you followed my message. Sorry it was a bit vague. Spirit boxes are completely bogus." I laughed but quickly quieted myself when I realized I was the only one laughing.

Brody let his eyes wander across my face, still silent.

"Are you okay? I'm sorry if I shocked you."

He met my eyes again before smiling. "You're absolutely stunning."

My own eyes grew large in shock. Had he called me stunning?

"Huh?" I asked, sounding, I'm sure, incredibly intelligent.

"I've never seen anything like you before," he went on, now looking me up and down.

It made me feel oddly vulnerable to have him studying me so closely, and I was suddenly very aware of every single fashion choice I'd made the day I'd died.

"I know I don't look very scary," I said, almost apologetically. "That's the problem with dying in a lame time period."

"This is… my mind is just blown," he said. It was almost as if he hadn't heard me, but I chalked that up to the shock. "I can't believe I'm talking to an actual ghost." He paused, shaking his head. "I have so many questions."

Chapter 12

My stomach dropped. He'd probably want to know about the afterlife. But giving away secrets was a big no-no. It was even worse than what I'd already done.

"You turned off all the cameras?" I asked. "And you're not recording anything?"

"I swear."

"I also need you to promise me you won't tell anyone about this."

Brody balked at this. I guess he hadn't anticipated being given a list of rules by a ghost.

"I'm actually the host of a paranormal investigation show on TV."

"Oh, I know all about that. It's my favorite show," I chimed in, trying not to sound too starstruck.

"You... watch my show?" he asked. "There are ghosts watching my show?"

I smiled at how excited this news made him. "It's not like we have much else to do on a Wednesday night."

"I can't believe this. I'm just absolutely in shock right now." He shook his head as he smiled. "And you!" He looked back at me again. "You are the most amazing thing I've ever seen!"

I knew he meant I was amazing because I was a ghost, but somewhere in my mind, I wanted to pretend he meant me as a person.

"If ghosts are real, why is this the first time I'm having a conversation with one?"

I winced. "Technically, I'm not supposed to be talking to you. It's sort of against the rules."

Brody's brows knitted together. "Am I going to get you in trouble? I don't want that."

"As long as we're careful, it should be fine," I said, feeling like this conversation suddenly felt much more intimate.

"Sorry, I'm so rude, I didn't even ask your name," he said, hitting himself on the forehead.

I'd already told him. But I could see why he wouldn't remember when he was distracted by seeing his first ghost.

"My name is Jane," I answered. "Jane Bridger."

"I'm Brody Specter," he said.

"I know," I answered in the dorkiest voice ever. Why was I like this? Why couldn't I keep my cool around a celebrity? "I've actually always wanted to know... is that your real name?"

He grinned. "Not buying it, huh?"

"It seems too perfect. Like those murder mystery authors whose last name is Slaughter," I said with a laugh.

"It's Brody O'Conner," he said with a slight wince. "But Brody Specter works better for the show."

"It is a bit more dramatic." I laughed.

This was unreal. I was laughing with Brody Specter. We were joking around like old buddies rather than joking around like a dead girl and a famous paranormal investigator. I stared at Brody for a moment longer before realizing how weird I was being. "Sorry... you had questions?"

He shook his head as if also being pulled from a trance. "So many. I'm actually not sure where to begin." He scratched his chin and pursed his lips. "Actually... I can't really remember any of them right at this moment. Go figure."

"Before we even start this whole twenty questions thing, I have to say I'm not really allowed to tell you much about the afterlife. I'm already breaking a lot of rules by talking to you."

"Not a problem. I'll take whatever I can get," he said.

"And I can't have you repeat any of this on your show," I added.

Brody held up three fingers. "Scout's honor."

My lips curled up into a smile. "Perfect. So, ask away."

"I mean… first off, I'm guessing you're the ghost I talked to at the Graumen's Chinese Theater?"

I nodded.

"Why were you there if this is your home base?"

Heat rose in my cheeks. I didn't really want to tell him why I was there, but I couldn't think of a lie fast enough. "I saw on the news you'd be investigating."

"Seriously?" His tone sounded flattered rather than horrified, so I chalked that up to a success.

"I'm a big fan. Did I mention that already?"

A grin broke out across Brody's face once more. "I'm sorry for smiling like an idiot. This is all blowing my mind. Not only am I speaking to a ghost in person, but that ghost is a fan? This day couldn't possibly get better. I'm half-expecting to wake up at any moment next to an empty bottle of cough medicine."

I couldn't believe Brody Specter was fangirling over me. While I was fangirling over him. There was an awful lot of mutual adoration going on in this room.

"I totally agree," I said after I'd taken a moment to mentally adapt to this new and impossible reality.

Brody kept his eyes trained on me, staring so intently I worried I'd gone into full haunt mode and made my eyes black or something. "I have a really weird question," he said after a moment. "Maybe the question itself isn't all that weird, it's just… it's going to sound weird."

I raised an eyebrow, slightly nervous about what he was about to ask me. "With a disclaimer like that, you'd better just ask your question, or I'll assume the worst."

Brody took a deep breath. "Can I touch you?"

I paused at his question. *Could* he touch me? I wasn't sure.

"Are you asking permission, or if it's possible?" I asked.

Brody thought this over for a moment. "Both?"

"I actually don't know if you'll be able to touch me," I answered. "This is the first time anyone's ever asked. Normally, if I accidentally run into someone out in the world, it just feels kind of funny. They can sense me, but they usually can't tell what it is."

I looked at my hands as if seeing them for the first time.

"I'm not sure what would happen if I let you touch me while I'm manifested," I said. "But I'd love to find out."

I refrained from saying, "I'd love to have you touch me," thinking that might come on a bit strong. And while I kept my cool externally, inside I was squealing.

"So, is it okay if I reach out and touch your hand?" he asked, seeming uncertain.

I would have thought that as a paranormal investigator he'd be ready for anything, but the fact that I'd agreed to let him touch me seemed to be throwing him off.

"Let's do it," I said, holding my hand out in front of me. I was probably even more curious than Brody about what would happen.

Brody slowly reached toward me. I tried to keep my hand steady, but it kept shaking. I was too nervous and excited for a poker face.

Just as our fingers touched, my entire hand felt warm. It was like I could feel the life in him. I smiled at the sensation, hoping he could feel it, too. I looked up to see a puzzled look on his face.

"What is it?" I asked. "Do you feel anything?"

"You're right," he answered. "It's just... sort of an odd feeling."

"Like a warmth?"

He shook his head. "No. It's more like... a tingling. A cold tingling." He looked a bit disappointed as he stared at our hands, but then he looked up and met my eyes. "Why? What does it feel like for you?"

I pushed my hand closer to him so it rested on his chest.

"It's warm," I said with a smile. "You don't get many opportunities to be warm as a ghost. This is nice."

Brody placed his hand over mine, and the warmth of him spread through me. It was an oddly comforting sensation.

But the spell was immediately broken by the sound of someone clearing their throat.

"Jojo," I groaned. But it wasn't Jojo. I looked over and saw William standing in the doorway, watching me with a furrowed brow. I pulled my hand away from Brody as quickly as I possibly could.

"Did you say Jojo?" Brody asked me, though I was hardly paying attention.

"William?" I said, looking over at an obviously shocked Victorian ghost.

"Terribly sorry to have interrupted," he said, his voice tight and proper. "I shouldn't have just popped by."

"Wait, I just—"

"Who are you talking to? Is everything okay?" Brody interrupted, obviously not able to see William since he hadn't manifested.

I ignored Brody in favor of standing up and running over to William before he could disappear.

"William, wait," I said, grabbing his hand just as he pulled himself from the room.

Chapter 13

My stomach dropped like I was on the Gold Rusher at Six Flags after downing a Squeezit. I had a spinning sensation in my head before the carpet under my feet was instantly replaced by hard stone.

The transition was jarring, but it was the least of my concerns in that moment.

"William, listen, that looked so much worse than it was," I said.

He pulled his hand from mine and began walking briskly away. The dark stone path led through large overgrown trees, and I only had a moment to wonder where William had taken us before I realized I was losing him.

"Hey, wait!" I called. "Will you just stop for a minute? I need you to listen to me."

"What?" he asked, turning on his heel so that I ran into him. After touching Brody's hand and going right through him, I'd almost forgotten that to William, I was an actual physical being.

Even though I could tell he was clearly upset, he still grabbed my arms to help me find my footing after I'd crashed into him.

"That wasn't what it looked like back there," I said.

As excited as I was to have met Brody, I was equally as upset I'd hurt William's feelings.

"And what did it look like?" William asked, his voice low and his eyes narrowed. "Were you talking to that glorified charlatan?"

"I wouldn't use the word charlatan… mostly because who even uses that word?" I said. "But yes, I was talking to him."

"And he could see you because you manifested to him." This wasn't a question, but I still felt the need to nod. "And you broke the rules and spoke to a paranormal investigator?"

"Wait a second," I said, holding up a hand. I may have been feeling contrite, but I wasn't about to let a double standard just waltz right past me. "You were literally just telling me we should talk to paranormal investigators. Now suddenly it's not okay because it was my idea and not yours?"

William let out a frustrated grunt. "That's not why it's not okay."

"Then what is it?" I asked. "Is it because he has a show? Or because he's famous? What?"

William pressed his lips together to form a hard line, staring at me for a moment and taking a few breaths before answering. "I don't trust him."

I pulled a face at this explanation. "Oh, I'm sorry. You don't trust him, or you don't trust me to be a good judge of character?"

William turned to walk away. I grabbed his arm and stopped him before he'd gotten more than two steps.

"Listen, I'm being careful, all right?" I said, my hand still holding his upper arm as I spoke. "I just wanted to connect with him. Hear his thoughts on the afterlife. I made him promise not to record anything."

"And you believed him?" William asked, the scoff obvious in his question.

"He's not going to film me, and he won't be passing on any of our conversation. He just wanted to know if ghosts were real." I loosened my grip on William's arm and let my hand slide down to his.

He looked down at our hands and seemed to hold his breath for a moment. I hadn't held his hand in an attempt to distract him, but it did seem to be working anyway. It was an unexpected perk.

The other unexpected perk was that I was actually enjoying our closeness as well.

William took a step closer to me, keeping his hand in mine. "I'm sorry to have gotten so upset," he said. "I just... I don't want you to be put in a bad situation. But I realize I was overstepping my bounds."

I let my thumb trace a circle in William's palm, shifting my weight forward so we were even closer. When I touched him, it wasn't the same as touching Brody. It didn't feel warm. But it wasn't a bad thing.

"Please promise me you won't tell Jojo about this," I pleaded.

William closed his eyes and sighed. "I won't tell him. But you have to stop meeting with paranormal investigators. I only have so much pull with Jojo. If he finds you out again, he might relocate you."

"Thank you so much," I said, relief flowing through me. I stood on my tiptoes and wrapped my arms around William's neck, pulling his body against mine. "I really appreciate it."

For a moment, William's body went stiff, as if he wasn't sure what to do about my hug. He didn't wrap his arms around me, but instead, stood there awkwardly.

"Is this how you hug?" I asked with a laugh, pulling away from him to see his shocked face.

"I've just... I've never really hugged before," he said. He must have read the confusion on my face because he quickly added, "Victorian era. Not a lot of touching. And... I mean... I never ended up getting married, so the most contact I had with my future bride was taking her hand to help her in and out of carriages or dancing with her."

I tried to suppress a smile but failed miserably.

"Are you laughing at me?" he asked. "You know, it's very rude to make fun of a dead man."

"I cannot believe you haven't hugged someone before."

"I've hugged my parents, obviously," he said, a sideways smirk on his lips. "But it just wasn't done when I was alive. At least, not often."

"Come here," I said, touching my hands gently to his waist before sliding them around to his back. "You can't just stand there, you have to hold me."

"Hold you?" he asked, his voice tight.

I rolled my eyes, though he couldn't see since I'd rested my head against his chest. "It's not a hug unless both parties are involved. Right now, this is more of a hostage situation."

"I suppose that makes sense," he said, though his voice still sounded wrong.

William wrapped his arms around me for a moment, and though it started out awkward, he eventually relaxed into it.

I kept my head resting on him while still embracing. "What do you think?"

"About what?" he asked, his voice sounding distant.

"This," I answered with a laugh. "Hugging. Do you feel like you've been missing out for the past hundred years?"

His arms tightened around my back. "It's nice." His voice sounded content. Almost dream-like.

"Everyone needs a good hug every now and then," I said, still holding him. "I made fun of you, but I don't really get many hugs anymore. You forget how much you miss physical contact with people until it's been twenty years between hugs."

He rested his head against the top of mine, and I could tell he was feeling more and more comfortable. "I honestly sort of forgot what it feels like to touch someone," he said. "It's not like I go around giving other ghosts hugs. That's something you don't necessarily consider—the stunning lack of physical contact in the afterlife."

"I guess that's not always the case, though," I said with a grin. "Jenny is constantly dating. Dying didn't slow down her love life at all."

William gave a soft laugh at this, his chest moving against me. After a moment, I reluctantly pulled away from him.

I hadn't expected to hug him now, or ever, but something about that contact was so comfortable. I hadn't realized how isolated I'd felt.

"Thank you for humoring me." I smiled.

How could I have missed how beautiful this guy was? I hadn't really noticed when I was being annoyed at him for trying to steal my TV family, or when I'd felt obligated to show him around. But when he smiled, his dimples stood out so prominently they changed his whole face. And his smile was wide. Wider than most people. It seemed like I could see all of his teeth when he smiled at me. It also didn't hurt that his gorgeous blue eyes crinkled in the corners.

But then I noticed he wasn't smiling anymore. He'd asked me a question, and I hadn't been listening.

"Sorry... what?"

This made him laugh, which only threatened to distract me again.

"I asked if I could show you around," he said. "I haven't been in this region long, but I found this place almost immediately and fell in love. It's my favorite spot so far."

"Yeah, I meant to ask you where we are."

"The Huntington Library, Art Museum, and Botanical Gardens," he recited, sounding a bit like a brochure.

"Huh," I responded, slightly puzzled. "I've never been here before, and I've been in this region for the past twenty years. Not to mention the fact that I grew up in California. How did I miss this place?"

"You never explore your own home," he said with a shrug. "I think that's true of most people."

He was probably right. If I hadn't died and, therefore, been stuck in the same area for the rest of eternity, who knows if I would have explored half of the places I'd seen in the afterlife? When you're stuck in Southern California for the rest of your death, it sort of forces you to explore. But in life, I probably would have taken it all for granted.

"Well, show me around! I hardly ever get to see a new

place."

William held out his arm as if he was my date to prom. It was a little cheesy, but I figured it was his deeply engrained chivalry from his time period, so I took it with a smile.

Chapter 14

"I'm not even sure where to start," William said, sounding like an excited little kid. "There's so much to see here. But I think we'll start with some art."

I think he was happy to be the one to show me around since I'd been showing him all of my favorite spots.

We walked to a large building that housed several rooms of paintings, sculptures, and pottery. Looking around the room, I suddenly felt incredibly uncultured. I had no idea what any of these paintings were. And unlike William, I'd spent my afterlife watching TV shows, attending concerts, and spying on celebrities.

"Did you know there are over 42,000 works of art here?"

My eyes widened. "Did you count them all?"

He laughed. "I'm not *that* bored. They mention that on the tours, which I've been on... too many times to count."

"Well, you should be great at showing me around then, huh?"

"I'll do my best. Just don't quiz me at the end of this, or I may fail miserably," he said, leading me over to a large bronze statue of a nude woman holding a bow and arrow. "This statue is my favorite piece at the Huntington." I tilted my head sideways as I studied it. "This is Diana. She was normally depicted one of two ways in the 18th century. Either nude while bathing, or fully clothed and hunting. This artist decided to combine the two, showing her during a hunt with nothing but a crescent moon in her hair. It makes her seem so... powerful, don't you think?"

I looked over at William as he stared at the statue with reverence in his eyes. "I was going to crack a joke about your favorite statue being a nude woman when you haven't even been hugged properly, but now I just feel bad," I said with a laugh. "You obviously know a lot about this piece. All I saw was a naked woman. I may need you to refine me a bit."

"I don't know if I'd call myself refined," he said, now looking over at me with that familiar and haunting smile.

"Hello? You're literally from the Victorian Era. I don't think you can live through that time period and not be refined."

"I don't know," he said. "My generation didn't have *The Fresh Prince of Bel-Air*."

"That's because you had an actual prince," I said before pausing. "Wait... you know about Fresh Prince?"

"You're not the only one who snuck in an occasional TV night in the afterlife." He gave me a knowing smile. "I may not be the media aficionado you are, but I still enjoy pop culture."

"I honestly never thought I'd be standing in the middle of an art exhibit with a dead man in Victorian clothing, talking about Fresh Prince." I shook my head. "This is a day that will go down in the history books."

"See, you're impressed by my knowledge of art, but art was the pop culture of my day. I'm sure you'd put me to shame when it comes to television programs."

He was trying to make me feel smarter than I was, and I appreciated it. "I'm just going to let you know right now no one calls them 'television programs.'" I giggled. "But it's super adorable you do."

I could see a faint blush rise to his cheeks. "I don't know that I've ever been referred to as adorable by anyone other than Jojo, but I'll take it."

We watched each other for a moment before I cleared my throat. "So… what's next on the grand tour?"

William shook his head, as if only just realizing he was supposed to be doing something. "Right. I think you'd probably enjoy the sculpture garden."

"Sculpture garden?" I asked. "That sounds oddly terrifying. Like a *Goosebumps* book I read once."

"I don't know what that is, but I do love a good ghost story."

William offered his arm once more. I took it embarrassingly quickly.

We left the art building and proceeded to a large, open lawn lined on each side with dozens of sculptures. It felt like they were watching us as we passed by, but I figured that was just my overactive imagination.

How was I constantly so creeped out by things when I was a ghost? I already knew what was out there. It was me.

"So, if you don't mind me asking, how did you die?" William asked, looking over with a raised eyebrow. "I know you mentioned your house burned down. Were you inside at the time?"

"Have I really not told you this?" That seemed weird. I'd talked to William about how he'd died. It seemed like I would have told him my story already. Asking another ghost how they died was basic small talk. Like asking your favorite color.

"You haven't. I didn't want to press you, but I've been curious. You look pretty young."

"You look pretty young too," I pointed out.

"I guess that's true. I was only twenty-five when I died."

"It's those fancy Victorian clothes. They make you look so much more mature," I said. "I guess my sunflower dress and combat boots don't exactly scream 'mature', do they?"

"I don't know. I'm quite fond of them." He grinned warmly, and my stomach tightened.

Keep it together, Jane. You're acting ridiculous.

"Okay, so... death," I said, trying to redirect the conversation.

William adopted a mock serious look on his face, though he couldn't completely hide his smile. "Yes... death."

"I was twenty-three and living in my parents' house, which I realize is super lame, but whatever," I said, waving this detail away. "They won some random trip to Ensenada from a contest they didn't even enter. The whole thing was way weird, and I'm still kind of confused about it. But that part isn't important."

I took a deep breath, realizing I was letting my words spill out all at once without really breathing. Not that I really needed to, I guess. Habit.

"So, my parents were out of town, and I was feeling super depressed because this cute guy had just stood me up for a date." William furrowed his brows. "Oh, don't worry. It wasn't a real date date. I'd only met him online. We exchanged info and stuff in a chat room, but this was going to be our first actual meeting."

"I was going to say that doesn't seem very romantic, but that's a bit hypocritical coming from someone who lived in a time of arranged marriages."

"See! Every generation is messed up in some way," I said, before continuing. "So, I waited for this guy for hours before finally giving up and stopping by Blockbuster to rent *Poltergeist*. I decided I'd make a night out of it and holed up in my room with the movie."

William stopped walking, pulled away from me, and looked me up and down. His eyes moved over my body, and I suddenly felt self-conscious. But I also didn't want him to look away. It was a weird mix of feelings. "So, this was your date outfit?"

I blushed, realizing he was trying to see what my idea of getting dressed up looked like.

"I know a sunflower t-shirt dress and combat boots probably doesn't really live up to the fancy gowns of the Victorian era," I said, suddenly feeling embarrassed.

"On the contrary. I was going to say this is much more comfortable and would probably allow you to actually enjoy a date," he said, his heart-melting smile returning. "My clothes aren't necessarily made for comfort."

"In my defense, I did wear my velvet choker. If that's not fancy, I don't know what is."

William brought his hand up to the choker, lightly tracing it with a single finger. The touch made goosebumps erupt down my arms. He lifted the pewter butterfly, studying it. "I like it." His fingers rested against my throat.

I swallowed hard, which he probably saw since we were so close, before saying, "Thank you," in a small voice.

His pulled away and continued walking. "So, what happened next?"

"Well, I fell asleep watching the movie and the next thing I know, the house is on fire, and I'm dead. It was super weird, because I hadn't left the stove on or anything."

"Couldn't you get out of the house?" he asked, sounding disturbed.

"I never woke up. And I'm still not sure why. I was literally passed out during the entire thing." I screwed my face up in frustration as I spoke. "I hadn't been drinking or anything, and I wasn't on any medication. I just sort of fell asleep and couldn't wake up."

"That seems a bit suspicious, doesn't it?"

I shrugged. "I guess, but I can't think of any way it could be foul play. Why would someone murder a random girl who still lived with her parents?"

"Did you ever find out what started the fire?" William asked, obviously going into sleuth mode.

"The fire department told my parents I'd left my curling

iron on," I said, giving William a meaningful look. "Do you see anything wrong with that theory?"

He studied me for a moment. "Your hair is straight?"

"Exactly!" I exclaimed, pointing at him for emphasis. "I always thought it was weird they said my curling iron was the source of the fire when I hadn't even used it for a few days." I paused, knitting my brows together. "I never really considered that me not waking up was sort of fishy, too."

"Honestly, the whole thing sounds odd to me," William said. "Maybe that's what your real unfinished business is. Finding out how you really died."

"Huh," I said simply, unsure of what to make of this theory. It did make sense, since I'd always wondered if I could really be stuck as a ghost because of an unreturned copy of *Poltergeist*.

"If you ask me, I think we need to investigate further," William said, giving me a matter-of-fact look.

I grinned, suddenly liking the idea of having more reasons to spend time together.

"I think you're right, Watson," I said.

He laughed, his dimples standing out prominently. "Why am I Watson?"

"Well, I'm obviously Sherlock. If you were more like Sherlock, you'd know that."

He laughed again, the sound giving me butterflies in my stomach.

"Touché," he said. "What's my first assignment, Sherlock?"

Chapter 15

"You said you grew up in Southern California, right?" William asked as we left the sculpture garden and wound our way through denser garden paths.

"Yeah, I did," I answered.

"So, can we go visit your childhood home?" he asked. "To investigate your suspicious death?"

I pursed my lips together. "I'm almost positive you're not allowed to visit your place of residence once you're dead," I said, trying to remember what I'd read in the rule book. "At least not if you still have relatives there."

William's eyes grew larger at this. "Do your parents still live there?"

I nodded. "Since I'm a Boon and not a Guardian, I can't go visit them."

"It's been so long since I was alive; I've forgotten rules like this," William said. "They aren't really applicable to me, so I've let them slip out of my mind."

We continued walking side by side through overgrown trees and bushes.

"I'm sorry you can't visit your parents," William said in a somber tone. "That has to be incredibly difficult."

"It was," I agreed. "But the longer I'm dead, the easier it is. They had to rebuild a lot of the house after the fire, so it never really felt the same, anyway." I looked at my black combat boots as we walked. "And in Jojo's defense, he let me visit them a few times right after I'd died, so I could give my parents a sense of peace and closure."

"That was kind of him," William agreed. "He's been known to bend the rules if he thinks someone truly needs it."

I paused. "Is that why you were able to transfer to California from England?"

William's jaw tightened, his eyes still trained on the ground. "I worry you might think me pathetic if I tell you why I was transferred."

"It can't be any more pathetic than being stuck in the afterlife because you didn't return a video to Blockbuster," I offered.

William stopped as we entered a rose garden. "It really can be, though."

I looked at him through my eyelashes, trying to pout my bottom lip. "Please?"

William narrowed his eyes before finally giving in. "Oh, fine." He slowly rubbed the back of his neck before continuing. "Jojo was worried about how... solitary I'd become."

I gave William a knowing look. "He thought you were too much of a loner?"

"More or less, yes. Though I don't see what's so bad about being a solitary ghost."

Jojo had said something similar to me a few years back, and suddenly, I wondered if he kept this close of tabs on the rest of his Boons. After all, he was in charge of a lot of ghosts. How did he have so much time to dedicate to William and me specifically?

"He mentioned he thought I'd fit in well with the Boons in the Southern California region and insisted I transfer," William said with a shrug. "Apparently, he knew we'd get on well."

William laughed, obviously joking, but his words made me wonder. Maybe Jojo really had been trying to set us up from the beginning.

"We must be his two favorite ghosts," I joked.

"Well, he does spend an awful lot of time with us when he should probably be busy with more important things."

"I guess we could be troublemakers. Maybe that's why we get so much special attention," I said.

William straightened his already perfect posture, tucking a strand of my hair behind my ear. "Speak for yourself. I am the perfect picture of decorum."

I could feel heat spring to life across my face and tried to distract him. "What do you miss the most about England?"

"Honestly? The tea," he said with a laugh, letting his hand fall away from my face.

"That has got to be the most British answer I've ever heard."

"That's why I spend so much time here," he went on, gesturing to the rose garden around us. "There's a tearoom in that building. And there are a few tables and chairs scattered throughout the rose garden so guests can enjoy an authentic English tea."

"So, you come and drink tea?"

"Even worse. I come and watch the living drinking tea. I'm trying to live vicariously through them." I opened my mouth to speak, but William instantly cut me off with a point of his finger. "Don't you dare make a 'dead joke' about me living vicariously through people."

I frowned. "How did you know that's what I was about to do?"

"I like to think I've started to pick up on some of your mannerisms."

"Oh, is that so?" I challenged.

"You get this goofy grin on your face when you've thought up some awful joke," he said.

"As if!" I protested, even though I knew he was right. "Wait... what other 'mannerisms' have you picked up on? I'm curious."

William's perfect smile returned. "You blush when you think you've revealed too much about yourself. And you laugh when you're nervous."

"What? I don't get nervous."

"Oh, you most certainly do. All the time."

"Okay, if you're so smart, what's your tell when you're nervous?"

"See, *I* can say with a surety I don't get nervous. And not in the way you just lied about it. I actually don't get nervous."

I raised an eyebrow. "Oh really? You don't get nervous?"

"I am made of stone."

"So, does that mean if I can figure out what your nervous tell is, I win?"

William raised an eyebrow at this. "Win what?"

I shrugged. "Bragging rights."

"Fair enough," he agreed. "If you can find my nonexistent tell for an emotion I don't experience, you get bragging rights."

I gave William a devilish grin. "Perfect. First thing's first, we have to make you nervous."

"As I said, it's impossible. I am the master and commander of my own emotions."

I narrowed my eyes as I studied William's stoic face. "So... you aren't scared of bugs? Or heights?"

"Hardly," he answered.

I pursed my lips together, and his eyes instantly darted to them before a faint blush rose in his cheeks.

Bingo.

Our hug earlier had definitely made him nervous. I took a step closer to William, so we were only inches apart.

"What are you doing?" he asked, his brow furrowed.

"I think you have something on your shoulder," I lied.

"Nice try. You're not going to scare me," he answered.

Poor boy. He thought I was going to jump scare him. He had no idea.

I slowly and deliberately laced my fingers through his.

With my free hand, I reached up and touched his cheek. His skin was cool under my fingertips as I leaned closer to him.

"Are... are you still looking at something on my shoulder?" His voice sounded small.

"Mhmm," I answered, leaning even closer to him.

I pressed my cheek against his for a moment, and when I moved back slightly, we were face to face, just looking at each other.

William's eyes darted to my lips, and this time it was my turn to blush. He slowly leaned forward and touched the tip of his nose to mine, closing his eyes.

I could feel his breath against my lips as my heart pounded in my chest. I had just wanted to make him nervous, but now that we'd started this, I didn't want it to stop.

William leaned forward that last few inches and gently placed his lips against mine. I thought for a moment about pulling away, but instead I returned the kiss, full of hesitation. We stayed like that for a moment before William pulled away and watched me intently, his brow furrowed as if wondering if what he'd done was okay.

I didn't answer him... not vocally, anyway. Instead, I pressed my lips to his again, tangling my free hand in his dark hair. He seemed frozen for a moment, but he slowly melted into the kiss. His lips were soft and warm as they moved over mine, and his arms wrapped around my waist, pulling me against him so that our bodies were flush. I could feel his heart hammering against mine, and it only encouraged me to continue.

William's fingers moved up my back as I parted his lips, deepening the kiss, my entire body sizzling with electricity.

How long had it been since I'd kissed anyone?

At least twenty years.

After what felt like an eternity, we pulled apart, both breathing heavily. My fingers were still tangled in William's dark hair, and his hands now resided on my lower back, still pulling me into him.

He stared at me with wide eyes, neither of us quite knowing

what to say. My whole body was shaking from the intensity of the kiss and the longing to be kissing him again.

William's hands moved absently across my back, and I wasn't quite willing to step away. I loved the feeling of my body against his. It had been so long since I'd had any sort of physical contact with anyone. It was like breathing after drowning. And I wanted to keep breathing.

I used every ounce of willpower I possessed to not kiss him again and instead, opted for my default coping mechanism: humor.

"I guess I win the bragging rights."

Chapter 16

William widened his eyes at my bad joke before letting a laugh escape his lips. Of course, this made me look down at his lips and wish I was still kissing him.

I refrained.

"I'm so sorry I don't have something terribly romantic to say to you. I just... wow." William's cheeks were red as he watched me intently.

"Wow is better than a bad joke," I offered.

William took one hand away from my back and brought it to my cheek. The action gave me chills, but I tried not to let him see it. His thumb traced my cheekbone. "I adore your bad jokes."

"Oh," I squeaked, doing an awful job of hiding my nervousness. "Good."

William leaned forward and pressed his lips to mine once more. It was only for a moment, but it was utter perfection.

"I want to show you something." He took my hand and pulled me away from the rose garden.

My mind was reeling from everything that had just happened. William and I had kissed. And it was his first kiss ever. How were we not talking about this? What could possibly be so important that he wanted to show me right now?

Or maybe this was his way of avoiding an awkward

conversation about our kiss.

"Okay, this is my favorite place in the entire Huntington garden," he said, still holding my hand in his and gesturing to the thick bamboo that surrounded us.

He was watching me with an eager grin, waiting to see how I'd react to the shoots that grew at least fifty feet high. It was definitely an impressive sight, but I still thought he'd chosen an odd moment to bring me here.

"Stay quiet for just a moment," he whispered, giving my hand a light squeeze.

I didn't want to admit it felt amazing to hold William's hand. It felt amazing to kiss him, too. And it wasn't because I was incredibly touch starved. I genuinely loved being around him.

"Do you hear that?" William asked.

"Hear what?"

"When the wind blows through the bamboo forest, you can almost hear whispering."

I closed my eyes, feeling my hair dance across my cheek as the wind picked up. As soon as it blew through the bamboo forest, I could hear the creak of the bamboo accompanied by a chorus of whispers.

I opened my eyes and smiled at William. "That's kind of creepy."

"I find it peaceful," he answered, returning my smile. Why did he have to have such an amazing smile? That wasn't fair. "I'm going to admit something, but you have to promise you won't make fun of me."

"I make no such promise." I stuck my chin out.

William rolled his eyes. "I feel like the veil between the living world and our world is thinner here. Like, this is the place where the two touch."

His words gave me chills, although that might have been because of the breeze that had just picked up a bit more. I heard the chorus of whispers in the bamboo forest again, and this time, I paid closer attention.

William was right. It wasn't just the sounds of the wind in the bamboo. It was whispering. I could almost make out words.

"That's not some trick of the wind?" I asked.

William smiled once more, knowing I'd heard it, too. "That's what I thought for a long time. But it's not just the whispering. You can feel it, can't you? Like this place is connected to everything."

I *could* feel it. But I wasn't sure I was ready to admit that.

"It definitely feels… different here," I said. "I can't put my finger on what it is."

William shook his head, concentrating once more. "It feels like this space isn't connected to the living world and our world alone, but perhaps to the one beyond ours as well."

What he was saying shouldn't have been scary, but it creeped me out. I'd always been kind of bad at being a ghost when it came to being spooked by supernatural stuff. It was pretty lame.

William leaned casually against the rail that separated the pedestrian path from the bamboo forest all around us. He still held my hand, which I'd almost forgotten he was doing until that moment.

Looking down at our entwined fingers, he frowned.

"Sorry if I crossed a line earlier." He ran his thumb lightly over my palm. "I've never… I mean… you know I've never kissed anyone. I didn't mean to make you uncomfortable or… take advantage. I just thought you were giving me… signs." His brow furrowed. "It was probably incredibly improper of me to be so assuming. And I never want you to feel uncomfortable around me. I should have asked you first, and I'm sorry about that."

He looked at his feet, letting go of my hand. The second he did, I missed the feeling of his hand in mine.

Now that I'd finally had contact with someone, I didn't want to give it up that easily.

William looked like he was about to start apologizing again, so I stepped forward, glad he was leaning against the railing, so we were closer to the same height.

I placed both of my hands against his chest, feeling his long-dead heart pounding there as he looked at me through his eyelashes. I slid my hands under his jacket so they were against the soft fabric of his white shirt, and I leaned in to him once more.

I could say that I was being kind and trying to stop his guilt and shame cycle, but I was being selfish. I wanted to kiss him again.

Oh man, did I want to kiss him again.

I pushed myself against him once more, loving that feeling of having someone hold me when I'd been solitary for so long. He didn't hesitate for even a moment to wrap me in his arms. This kiss was less reserved than our first. The first kiss was like a question. William was asking me if this was okay.

Now that I'd given him my answer, he let go of his deeply ingrained social niceties and dissolved into me, pressing his lips firmly against mine.

His fingers traced my sides, my waist, my hips, and finally crept up my back to pull me close. For someone who hadn't been touched in so long, it felt amazing to be this close to William.

I breathed him in as his fingers dug into me, my own hands still on his chest. I could feel my heart pounding, despite the fact that my heartbeat was completely useless in death.

That was how good the kiss was.

When we breathlessly broke apart for air, I let myself collapse against his neck as he wrapped both arms around my back protectively.

"Now, do you see how unnecessary your apology was?" I asked, a bit embarrassed by how breathless I was.

He inhaled deeply, his chest rising against mine. When he exhaled, it was shaky.

"I'm still very new to this," he said, that familiar smile in his voice.

"For someone so new, you're amazing at it." I pulled away just enough to look at him, letting him keep his arms around me and never wanting him to move them.

"Well, that's a bloody relief," he said, before his eyes widened at his apparent profanity. "Sorry. Caught up in the moment."

"I don't think the Victorian swearing police are going to come after you. It's okay." I laughed.

A content smile spread over his lips. "I definitely didn't see the evening going this way. Especially with how it started."

I felt my stomach drop at the mention of my rule-breaking time with Brody.

"You have to know Brody and I were just conducting some paranormal experiments," I said, my brow furrowing. "I wasn't trying to break any rules. He wanted to learn more about our plane of existence, and I was... helping."

William looked at the ground before biting his lip.

Why did he have to keep doing things with his lips? It wasn't helping my concentration at all.

"I'm not going to tell Jojo," he promised. "But I really want you to be careful. I realize I'm sounding an awful lot like a jealous beau right now, but even with my feelings for you aside, I get an odd sense from him."

I wanted to focus on the implication that Brody had ulterior motives, but I couldn't stop the smile that crossed my face. "My beau?" I asked with a laugh.

William's cheeks flushed slightly, though a grin appeared. "Don't try to change the subject," he warned in his deep voice. "I mean it. Mr. Specter worries me. There's just something... off about him."

"Well, he's a performer, so it makes sense," I said dismissively, not wanting to promise him I'd stay away from Brody if I couldn't keep that promise. "Let's go back to the interesting part. What exactly is a beau?"

"I'm not making any assumptions about the two of us," he began. "I'm simply calling myself an interested party."

I grinned, lowering my voice to a whisper. "I like that." I gave him one last long, slow kiss before regretfully pulling away. "Interested suitor or not, I should probably head back home."

William straightened, his brows knitting. "Must you?"

I adopted my best British accent—which was awful, by the way—and said, "I must."

He took my hand, bringing my palm up to his lips to place a gentle kiss there as his blue eyes roamed over my face.

Why was I suddenly unable to resist the man who had driven me crazy only days before?

Leaning forward, I planted another kiss on his lips. "One for the road," I whispered with a wink, pulling my hand away from his and disappearing from the bamboo forest before he could react.

I appeared a second later in my room in the abandoned Ramona house. Taking a deep breath, I flopped onto my bed, a grin involuntarily spreading over my face.

Closing my eyes, I turned my head to the side, only to open them once more to see Jojo lying on the bed next to me with a matching grin, chewing gum.

"Did my matchmaking work?" he asked. "Tell me everything."

Chapter 17

"Boundaries, Jojo!" I yelled, throwing my arms out and accidentally catching him square in the face.

"Ow! You broke my nose!" he whined, even though I knew I hadn't.

"It serves you right for popping into bed with me," I told him, sitting up and shaking my head.

"Well, when you say it like *that*," he said, rolling his eyes. "Don't make it weird, Jane. I wanted to have some pillow talk about your new British boyfriend."

I raised my eyebrows. "Jojo, I don't think 'pillow talk' means what you think it means."

He scoffed at this. "Um, excuse me, but I'm a centuries-old being with higher intelligence who's in charge of the afterlife and many other important endeavors. I think I know what words mean."

"It's an intimate conversation you have in bed after an intimate moment," I explained. Jojo continued to look at me like this didn't faze him at all. "An *intimate* moment, Jojo," I emphasized.

"What's more intimate than two besties sharing some hot gossip?"

"Oh my gosh, I swear, if I have to spell it out for you, I might die all over again from embarrassment."

Jojo scrunched his face up, trying to understand my meaning.

I could tell the exact moment it hit him, because he suddenly burst out laughing. "That's fantastic," he said. "And while I do find you quite fetching, I'm much too busy to be tied down by the likes of you." Jojo then adopted a smug look as he continued. "Besides, I've got my eye on someone else."

"Jenny?" I asked, my interest now piqued.

"Sadly no," he said. "Someone a bit more… living."

My eyes widened. "Jojo Marie… whatever your last name is!" I exclaimed. "You have a crush on a living girl?"

"First of all, it's Akahata, which means 'supreme' because… well, look at me," he gestured to himself. "And second—"

"Wait, your name is Akahata?" I asked. "How did you get Jojo out of that?"

He shrugged. "I thought Jojo would be easier for all the white people in the afterlife. You guys are awful with non-Anglo-Saxon names."

"I mean, you're not wrong," I admitted. "So, what's your real middle name? I'm assuming it's not Marie?"

"I don't have a middle name," he stated simply. "Or a last name, actually. That wasn't a thing in New Zealand back in my day."

"Oh," I said, still slightly off-balance that the Jojo I'd known my whole afterlife was actually named Akahata. "Well, as much as I appreciate the history lesson, I want to know who this girlfriend of yours is."

I expected Jojo to change the subject back to William and me, but instead he flopped onto his belly on the bed beside me again. He cradled his chin in his hands and kicked his feet up behind him like a gossip-y teen in a 1950s movie.

"Okay, so, her name is Vesper Parrish, and she lives in Concord, Massachusetts," he began, smiling as he spoke. "She has peach hair and two sisters, one of whom is a really nice girl."

"Wait, you've spoken to this girl you like?" I gawked. "You're such a hypocrite! You said that wasn't allowed!"

"I haven't spoken to *her*," he corrected. "I've spoken to her sister."

"How is that better?" I asked.

"Because her sister is dead," he said, as if this should be obvious. "Well, that's not entirely true. She died once. She's alive now. It's a whole thing."

I pulled a face. "I am so confused."

Jojo shrugged. "I'm pretty sure Vesper is a witch?" He said this like a question. "Is that a real thing? I'm still not positive on that. But the fact that they're different means I can sort of contact them and not feel too guilty about it."

"Bending the rules for your favorites?" I asked, raising one eyebrow at Jojo as I nudged him with my shoulder. "It seems like that might be something you do often."

"Ooooh yeah, you and William figured that out, did you?" he asked. "I'm sorry I'm such a good matchmaker, but I shipped you guys long before I moved him to the Southern California region."

"You've been planning this for that long?" I asked, unable to believe it.

"I've been keeping an eye out for someone suited to William for ages. Long before you even died. But no one was good enough for him. After you died, I was pretty sure you were the one, but I needed some time to properly vet you."

He said all of this in such a matter-of-fact way that I almost didn't question him. Almost.

"Don't you have better things to be doing in the afterlife?" I asked. "I feel like you're hosting *Singled Out* when you're supposed to be keeping tabs on millions of Boons."

Jojo gave a little gasp and placed his hand dramatically to his chest, clutching imaginary pearls. "Excuse you, I'm much more stylish than Jenny McCarthy. Do you not see this turn-of-the-century top I paired with some cowboy boots that were worn by Wyatt Earp? I am an icon."

"Can't argue with that," I said. "But seriously, how do you have so much time to play dead-person-matchmaker and find yourself a totally inappropriate love interest at the same time?"

"Well, William's been dead since the 1800s and you've been dead twenty years, so it's not like I put this thing together overnight."

"I guess that's fair," I said. "But I still don't know how I feel about you orchestrating my love life."

Jojo rolled his eyes. "Don't worry about it. If you don't like him, then you don't have to feel pressured to pursue that romantic avenue. It's not a big deal! I'll just be eternally crushed and feel like my death's work has all been for nothing. No sweat."

"Oh good. Thanks, Jojo," I said, injecting as much sarcasm into my voice as I possibly could.

"And my innocent little crush on Vesper isn't inappropriate at all. Except for the fact that she's alive. Just ignore that part. And the fact that she might be a sociopath." He winced. "Scratch that. She's definitely a sociopath. But such a pretty one. Also, I'm kind of scared of her. But in a good way."

I rolled my eyes. "Men."

"Says the girl who got home in the middle of the night with a huge grin on her face. Spill it, sister!"

"I am *so* not discussing my love life with you," I said.

"Fine. I'll go ask William. He'll tell me," Jojo said, staring at me intently.

I wasn't taking the bait. "Go ahead."

Jojo sighed. "You're no fun," he said before he disappeared from my room.

Despite everything Jojo had just told me, the grin reappeared on my face as my mind wandered to William and that toe-curling kiss we shared in the bamboo forest.

I was already in so deep.

***

I'd spent the next day wondering what ghost etiquette was after a "sort of" date. It's not like William could call me since we didn't have phones. And I didn't want to be the one to go see him. I wouldn't actually even know where to go. William haunted the Johnston house, but that wasn't his home base. Maybe he used the Huntington for that?

There was a lot I didn't know about this guy I was suddenly smitten with.

I was preparing to pop over to the Huntington bamboo forest, just to see if William was there, when I heard a knock at the door.

Jenny, who had been lying on the couch in the living room texting no one in particular looked over at me.

"Did someone knock on our door?" she asked.

I shrugged. "This house is so obviously abandoned. It's not like a solicitor would come here, right?"

As the handle turned, we both stared in nervous anticipation.

"Jane?"

Brody Specter walked into the house slowly, looking uncertain. The contrast between Brody and William was almost laughable. Where William was reserved and meticulously put together, Brody was the walking embodiment of the hot "bad boy" stereotype. His black leather jacket and ripped jeans were so different from William's well-tailored suit.

I missed William.

"OMG, girl! It's your celebrity boyfriend," Jenny said, squealing.

Suddenly, I was glad Brody couldn't see us.

"What is he doing here?" I asked.

"Coming to get some sweet ghost action, probably," Jenny said, making a kissy face at me.

"Jojo will kill me if he finds Brody here."

"Is he coming over tonight?" she asked.

"Oh yeah, in fifteen minutes. He told me he'd be here right at 8:30," I said sarcastically. "Since when does Jojo ever tell us his plans to come over?"

"Never?"

"Exactly!" I said, a bit panicked now. "He just shows up at

the least inopportune times."

"Jane?" Brody said again.

"Um, correction. When *you're* doing something wrong," Jenny said. "I am perfect. Jojo can't be mad at me for anything."

"Since you're such a perfect friend, will you please go distract him?" I begged. "He can't see Brody here."

"Then get rid of Brody," she said matter-of-factly.

"Jenny, please?" I asked again.

Jenny sighed. "Girl, this friendship is too one-sided. As payment for all I do for you, I expect some gossip in return later on, okay?"

"Anything you want."

Jenny got off the couch slowly, looking like it took all of her strength as she dramatically put her phone in her pocket. "If Jojo isn't at his house, then I don't know what to tell you."

"If you can't find him, just let me know, and I'll get rid of Brody."

Jenny gave me a mock salute before disappearing from the room. As soon as she did, I tried my best to regain my focus and concentrate on manifesting to Brody. It took several attempts before I was able to do it, but when I finally did, Brody looked just as shocked as the first time.

"Jane?" he asked, his honey brown eyes wide as he stood stock still.

"In the flesh," I said. "Sort of."

Really, Jane? Really? You had to do one of your lame jokes in front of Brody?

To my astonishment, Brody actually laughed at the terrible joke, immediately putting me at ease.

"Sorry. I do that a lot," I explained, looking at my feet.

"I love it. At least you know your sense of humor is alive and well," he offered, making his own lame death pun.

Of course, I laughed because he was speaking my love language, but I felt a twinge of guilt as William came to mind.

"What are you doing here?" I asked.

"I wanted to see you again," he said, looking shy.

I'd never seen him look shy before. It was oddly adorable.

"Did you bring any cameras?" I asked. Mostly because I had to. I was already in enough trouble for talking to Brody. I didn't need our conversation plastered all over the world wide web.

"Not even one," he reassured me, a smile engulfing his face.

Brody Specter was smiling at me. Brody Specter wanted to see *me*. Had I died again and gone to fangirl heaven?

"I was just worried about you after our last conversation," he said, taking a step toward me. "You left so fast and... you looked really worried. Did that Jojo person hurt you?"

"Jojo?" I asked, wondering how he even knew that name.

"Yeah, you said Jojo before you left." He paused. "Well, you said 'Jojo' and then 'William' I guess."

As he spoke, I remembered exactly how the incident had played out, and I had to stop myself from hitting my own forehead. "That's right. Sorry for the confusion. I thought it was Jojo, but someone else had popped into the room."

Someone else? William wasn't "someone else." He was William. My William. Sort of.

"Gotcha. I'm glad you're okay," Brody said with another smile. "So, who is Jojo?"

He seemed oddly fixated on Jojo before I remembered I hadn't really told him who William was, so he only had Jojo's name to go off of. "Jojo is my friend," I said, my smile slightly strained. I didn't want to give too much away about the afterlife. No need to dig my second grave deeper than it already was.

"Is he like... your superior or something? You seemed upset when you thought it was him."

"He's harmless." I laughed, trying to imagine anyone describing Jojo as "superior" other than himself. "He's in charge, but he's not scary. He's basically a big teddy bear."

Brody nodded. "So, the afterlife is like... a corporate job, basically? Like, you have a boss, and he has a boss and everything?"

"Dude, I have no idea! And that's the frustrating thing!" I began, excited to vent to someone new. "You think you don't know anything when you're alive? It's even more confusing once you're dead." I shook my head before continuing, completely abandoning my resolve to not give anything away. "Like, this isn't even the final step in the afterlife, apparently. And this isn't the only thing you can do in this step. It's totally bananas."

"Really?" Brody asked, still watching me intently. "So, there's... an after-afterlife or something?"

I shrugged. "I guess. That's the word around town, at least."

"Huh," he said simply. "That's so weird. And not at all what I excepted the afterlife to be like."

"Right? It's a weird adjustment when you get over here. You have to reassess everything you thought you knew."

Brody furrowed his brow as he looked at the ground, deep in thought. Had I broken him with all of these revelations?

"So, if there's another afterlife after yours, can you contact that one the way I'm contacting you right now?"

I opened my mouth to tell him there wasn't, but quickly closed it again, remembering my night with William. "Actually," I began, before trailing off.

"Actually, what?" Brody asked, hanging on my every word.

It felt nice to have him so invested in what I was saying. Never in a million years had I thought I'd become friends with Brody Specter. And yet, here we were. Having a conversation.

"There is a place I recently learned about where the veil between all the planes seems... thinner," I said, before backtracking. "More accessible, is maybe a better term."

Brody smiled. "That sounds like an amazing place to do some paranormal investigation." He shook his head as if imagining it right at that moment. "I wonder if I'd be able to catch EVPs from your plane and the next."

"I bet you could!" I exclaimed, my face lighting at the prospect of helping Brody with his paranormal investigation. It was like all of my fangirl dreams were coming true. Except that I was dead and wouldn't actually be able to be on his show.

"Do you think you could show me where it is?" he asked, his

eyes so full of hope I almost didn't feel the way my heart sank.

I wasn't supposed to be talking to Brody, let alone telling him where to find the secrets of the afterlife.

Plus, that was my spot with William. That was our place. I may have been a huge dork with a celebrity crush when it came to Brody Specter, but I had an actual real crush on William. I didn't want to sully our place by taking another guy there.

"What's wrong?" Apparently, my face was betraying me as Brody stared.

"Nothing," I answered quickly. "I just… I don't think I'm really supposed to show you that place."

His face fell and, even though my crush on him had been dampened significantly by the gorgeous Victorian ghost I'd kissed, I still felt guilty for letting him down. But how could I possibly take him to the bamboo forest? How could I betray William like that?

"I don't want to get you into any trouble," Brody said, shifting his weight and giving me a forced smile. He was obviously upset I wasn't going to take him. "Don't worry about it, okay? It's not that big of a deal."

That face. The puppy dog eyes. All of it. I could feel the guilt pouring over me like a cold ocean wave slapping me in the face.

"I mean… maybe I could show you once," I began, regretting the words even as I was saying them. What would William think? But the way Brody's face lit up made some of my guilt die down.

His eyes widened. "Really? You'd seriously do that? That would be amazing!"

Now it was my turn to force a smile. What had I gotten myself into? I really did want to help Brody, but I also didn't want to do anything that would put my relationship with William in jeopardy again. And William wasn't exactly Brody's biggest fan.

"You have no idea how much this means to me," Brody said.

Maybe one quick trip wouldn't hurt. William would never know. I'd show Brody where to do his research, and then I'd cut ties with him so I didn't risk any future damage to my relationship.

"No problem," I said, wringing my hands and realizing this was the second stupidest thing I'd ever done, after not waking up when my house was on fire.

Chapter 18

I stood in the middle of the bamboo forest at the Huntington with my eyes closed. My spot. My spot with William. The spot I'd told Brody about, like a total dummy.

I was supposed to meet Jenny and Jojo at the police station to do some digging on my untimely death, but I just had to pop over to the bamboo forest first. I had to make sure it really was the spectral portal I thought it was. Otherwise, I'd potentially damaged my relationship with William for no reason.

It was nearly six in the morning and the wind had died down, but even in the stillness, I could hear the whispers.

The tall bamboo stood stock still in the cool night, making the whispers that much creepier. If it wasn't the wind making the sound, William's theory had to be right. The bamboo forest was somehow connected to the *other* other side.

I needed to get off the path and into the actual forest if I wanted to find answers, and I was running out of time before my meeting. Stepping over the railing that divided the pathway from the bamboo forest, I looked around to make sure no one was watching. Of course, I quickly realized not only was The Huntington closed right now, but also, I was dead, and no one would be watching me, anyway.

Force of habit.

I let my fingers trail across the tall bamboo as I walked

through the forest, listening as the whispers seemed to get louder.

Following the noise, I stumbled into a bare clearing in the forest. And not just a space where the bamboo was sparse, but a completely barren area. The ground looked almost scorched in the shape of a perfect circle large enough for several people to stand in. I furrowed my brow, wondering how this area could exist in such a meticulously maintained garden.

Kneeling, I placed my hand against the earth, and my fingertips instantly tingled.

Had I done it? Had I found some kind of window to the next section of the afterlife?

"Jane?"

I fell face first onto the ground at the shock of hearing William's voice beside me. It only took a moment for me to stand up and brush myself off, but I was already wishing I could die again just to get out of facing him after that not-so-graceful moment.

"William!" I said brightly.

Too brightly.

"What are you doing out here?" he asked, his smile wide as he approached me.

He stopped just short of me, as if suddenly wondering how to proceed after our amazing few kisses the last time we were together.

I wasn't exactly sure what to do, either. I wanted to kiss him again, but were we at that point?

I thought dying would have gotten me out of awkward dating situations, but it turned out I was just as awkward in death as I was in life.

"I was thinking about what you said about the bamboo forest being some kind of... what would you call it?" I asked.

"Maybe a thinner part of the veil between planes?" he offered, raising his eyebrows at me.

"Yeah, that!" I said. "So, I was hoping to dig a little deeper into that and—" I gestured to the scorched earth around me.

William looked it over, not seeming to understand why this was particularly interesting.

"Listen," I told him.

He watched me for a moment before his smile returned. "The whispers are louder here," he said.

"Exactly." I smiled. "I think your theory was right. And I think this spot is the source of the whispers."

William nodded before focusing on me. "And what sparked this sudden interest in investigating?"

My stomach knotted. I definitely wasn't going to tell him I'd been talking to Brody Specter. And there was no way I'd let him know I was thinking of bringing Brody to the place where William and I had shared that totally amazing kiss. I already regretted agreeing to take Brody here. I wanted desperately to get out of it, but wasn't sure how.

So instead, I changed the subject. "Well, Jojo gave me permission to investigate my death a bit more," I offered. "I guess it got me into the investigative mood."

William grinned. "So, the game is afoot?" he asked, his British accent making the declaration that much better.

"Yes, Watson," I said. "And if you're not too busy, I could use all the help I can get."

William slid his hand into mine, instantly reminding me of how close we'd been in this location not too long ago.

"You lead the way," he said, nearly killing me all over again with his perfect dimples.

I took a deep breath, mostly to recover from the brilliant grin, and partially to focus on where I wanted to bring us.

"We're heading to the police station. Jojo thinks I can find something there that will help me figure out my death."

"Well, I'm honored to be along for the ride."

I closed my eyes to transport us to where we needed to be.

A moment later, we both stood in a quiet dark room within a police station. William looked around curiously as he dropped my hand.

I hated the feeling of not holding his hand.

"So, what exactly are we looking for? I'm not much of a detective, I'm afraid," he said.

"I thought Jojo and Jenny would be here already," I said. "But I think we're a bit early."

I walked around the room, glancing at labels on various boxes and alphabetized filing cabinets.

"If my extensive knowledge of movies and TV shows is correct, I should have a file in one of these cabinets," I said. "And inside should be a super flattering picture of me as well as tons of evidence that points us in the direction we want to go."

William scrunched his nose at this.

"Yeah, it didn't sound convincing in my head either," I said with a laugh. "I guess we just see if there's anything suspicious in my file. And if there's not, I really am an idiot who burned her house down with a curling iron she didn't even use."

William gently placed his hand on my back. "I think we'll find some much-needed answers today." He smiled, making my cheeks warm just as Jojo and Jenny appeared in the room.

"Girl, you're lucky ghosts can't get dusty, because I am so not down with this dank place," Jenny said, lifting her lip at the overcrowded shelves around her.

"That's the spirit, Jenny," Jojo said, looking between William and me with a wide smile.

William instantly dropped his hand from my back.

"I'm sorry if we're interrupting anything," Jojo said, his eyes bright and mischievous. "Actually, that's a lie. I hope we were interrupting something. Otherwise, this is a Saturday wasted."

I rolled my eyes. "Jojo, you're dead. Days of the week don't matter anymore."

"This is coming from the girl who invades my territory every Wednesday night to watch her ghost show," William teased.

Jojo made a sound somewhere between a squeal and a cry. "It's happening! Jenny, it's happening," he said, looking over at Jenny, who was already glued to her phone again. Jojo didn't seem fazed by her lack of enthusiasm. "They're falling in love!"

"Jojo, would you knock it off?" If my cheeks hadn't been red before, they definitely were now. "We have an important mission."

Jojo straightened with a nod. "Right you are. It's time to figure out what cold-hearted, jealous rodeo queen or theme park princess killed you."

I shook my head. "What are you on about now?"

He simply shrugged. "It seems like a better story than whatever we're bound to find."

"Truth," Jenny said, still not glancing up from her phone.

With a sigh, I pulled out my file and rifled through the papers inside.

"Why do we all need to be here for this?" Jenny asked.

"Because, sweet Jenny," Jojo began, "Jane needs moral support, and we've got nothing better to do."

"Are you sure you don't have anything better to do, Jojo?" William asked. "You are in charge of every Boon in the afterlife, you know."

"I see what you're getting at. You're trying to get us to leave so you and Jane can have some grown-up alone time," he said, and I could practically hear the eyebrow waggle in his voice.

A dull thud sounded behind me, which I assumed was William hitting Jojo on the arm, but I was too busy pulling my file from a dusty box to care.

"You know what I just realized?" Jojo said. "All of us have 'J' names, except poor William over here. And if we're going to start a synth pop band, that just won't stand."

"Jojo, could you not be quirky for like, two seconds?" Jenny whined. "I swear it's like talking to the lovechild of Zooey Deschanel and Jeff Goldblum."

"Guys," I said, interrupting what I'm sure would have been an epic showdown between Jenny and Jojo. "I found something kind of weird."

"Is it Jenny's addiction to a phone that doesn't work?" Jojo asked, holding his hand up for a high five no one gave him. He dropped his hand in a huff. "I'm unappreciated in my time."

"The police took down some testimonies from neighbors

and things after the fire. I think they were trying to determine if it was arson," I began, ignoring Jojo's antics like I normally did. "And this guy, who said he lived nearby, told police he'd heard my parents telling me to unplug the curling iron before I left the house on numerous occasions."

I looked over at Jojo and William, who were both watching me. Jenny was still on her phone.

"So… you were as forgetful in life as you are in death?" Jojo asked.

"No," I answered. "My parents literally never said that to me once. I hardly ever used my curling iron. And when I did, I always turned it off."

"Why would that man lie about that?" William asked.

"Right?" I answered. "That seems suspicious."

I looked at the testimony. The photo showed a man in his mid-30s with short jet-black hair, defined cheekbones, and dark eyes, wearing a priest's collar.

"Father Hawthorne," I said, my eyes narrowed as I read the name on his testimony. "I didn't know of any priests living in our neighborhood, but I guess I could have missed that. I wasn't the most social person."

"But I imagine you would have noticed a man in priest's attire walking outside of your home often," William said. "He must have passed by often if he claimed to hear your parents talking to you so many times."

My mind raced as I tried to figure out what this all meant. "Why would a priest lie about something so minor? That seems weird, right?"

"Maybe he mistook you for someone else?" Jojo said, offering his first serious contribution to the situation.

"Maybe," I said, my voice distant.

Something wasn't adding up. The testimony had probably seemed insignificant to the police. There weren't really any red flags in it for someone who didn't know me. But the fact that my death had ultimately been deemed an accident by police with my curling iron being the source of the fire made this statement incredibly suspicious.

I hadn't used my curling iron. I knew that for a fact. And yet it had started the fire that had killed me. Then there was the fact that I hadn't woken up after the fire had started. Would the coroner have looked for any drugs in my system if the fire was ruled an accident? Was there even enough of my body left to test?

But who could have drugged me? None of it made any sense.

"Why is the hot priest in your file?" Jenny asked, looking over my shoulder at the witness testimony in my hands.

"Jenny, this is neither the time nor the place," Jojo said with a disapproving *tsk*.

"What are you talking about, dude?" she asked. "That man right there is the hot priest I dated a while back."

I glanced down at the picture again before meeting Jenny's eyes. "This guy is the hot priest?"

"I mean… he probably has a real name, but yeah. Hot priest basically sums him up," Jenny said. "He looked exactly like that when I dated him, too."

I shook my head. "Does that mean he died around the same time? If he'd died later, he would have looked older when Jenny went out with him."

"You dated this man after you died?" William asked. "And you're sure it's him?"

Jenny narrowed her eyes at the picture again and grinned. "Oh yeah. That's him. I couldn't forget those cheekbones if I tried."

"Okay, keep it together, Jenny," Jojo said. "Was this guy a Boon? Because I definitely don't recognize him."

Jenny shrugged. "I don't know. He didn't say. I guess he could have been a Guardian, but he didn't have those fancy wings."

"How did you even meet him?" Jojo asked. "How do you meet any of your conquests?"

"Most of them I run into while haunting," she said. "But this guy I met at a church. He must have been hanging around because… you know… the whole hot priest thing?"

We all looked back down at the picture. Something was definitely off.

"He's not a Boon," Jojo said definitively. "I may not be great at my job, but I know all of my Boons."

"How do we find out who he is?" I asked. "It can't be a coincidence some random guy gave the police false information about my death and then turns up and dates Jenny twenty years later."

"Did the two of you actually go somewhere on your date?" William asked. "Did you leave the church and appear somewhere else together?"

Jenny scrunched up her face. "No. We just hung around in the church and talked. It was pretty boring. He wanted to know more about who I hung out with and stuff." She shrugged. "If he wasn't so good looking I wouldn't have stuck around."

William watched Jojo with concern in his eyes. "Is it possible this man isn't dead? If Jenny never saw him appear in a new location the way we can… could he be a living person who can see the dead?"

"He wouldn't be the first," Jojo answered.

"But Jenny said he looked exactly like this. I don't care what skin care you use, no one can look exactly the same for twenty years."

"Except Paul Rudd," Jojo said.

"Except Paul Rudd," I agreed.

"Let me ask Seraph if he knows who he is," Jojo said.

"Seraph?"

"He's one of the head honchos over the Guardians."

"And his name is 'Seraph'?" I asked skeptically. "Isn't that a little… on the nose?"

"Yeah, those guys are so dramatic. They've got their wings and their angel names like they're so high and mighty," Jojo said with a roll of his eyes. "Everyone knows Seraph's name was Will when he was alive. Nice try, angel boy."

"Well said, Akahata," I answered.

Jojo pointed a finger at me. "Don't even try to compare me to those drama queens. I changed my name to be more accessible to *you* people." He gestured to the three of us gathered in the room. "The culturally challenged. If anything, I should be commended for trying to be less dramatic."

"Jojo, you're literally wearing the same outfit Freddie Mercury wore," I reminded him, gesturing to the white pants and shirt with the bright yellow jacket.

"And I'm slaying it," he stated. "Do you want my help or not?"

"Yes, please. It would be so rad to find out that my unfinished business doesn't have to do with Blockbuster."

"Then tell me you like my jacket," Jojo said.

I would have tried to argue with him, but I knew he was serious. Me finding out about my death might actually hinge on admitting I liked Jojo's jacket. This was a literal life or death situation.

"I like your jacket, Jojo," I said, my voice as monotone as I could possibly make it.

"This old thing?" he asked, feigning modesty. "You're too sweet."

"You'll let us know what you find out?" William asked, attempting to get Jojo back on track.

"Sure will, lover boy," Jojo said, winking at William and once again making me blush. "Stay fresh, cheese bags! I'll talk to you soon."

And with that, he disappeared.

Chapter 19

I was distracted during my routine haunts that next night. I kept wondering who the man in the police file was and why he would have falsified information regarding my death. Then there was the troubling fact that he'd somehow had a conversation with Jenny when we weren't sure he was dead.

Was that even possible?

I sat on my bed in the old Ramona house, twisting my smiley face ring around on my finger. Jojo was supposed to be here by now, but he still hadn't shown up. What if the hot priest was some sort of demon who'd killed him a second time? Were demons even a real thing?

"Jane!" Jojo said loudly from the living room. His voice was whiney as I heard his footsteps nearing my room.

At least he wasn't dead again.

"What took you so long?" I asked. "I was worried the hot priest had killed you."

Jojo cocked his head to the side at my comment before putting his hand up against my forehead. "You know I'm already dead, right? Have been since the 1500s."

"I mean dead again… or something," I said. "Shut up. Don't mock me. Just be happy I was worried about you."

"I shall take that as the highest of compliments," he said, fluffing up his gray curly pompadour and taking a seat beside me on the bed. "So, I have to ask you something."

I sat up straighter, ready to get into whatever he'd found out about Father Hawthorne. "Go for it."

"Do you think Jenny has a thing for me?" he asked, completely catching me off guard. "She keeps asking to hang out, and while I'm super flattered, I don't think that can happen."

Jenny had been hanging out with Jojo because I'd kept asking her to keep him distracted. If he was starting to notice how often she wanted to spend time with him, he might also figure out that I'd been meeting with Brody Specter after he asked me not to.

"I think she enjoys your company," I began slowly. "I mean, she puts on a show of being really confident and secure, but I think she wants to have a friend. And you are really easy to get along with. You're so nice and funny and understanding..."

I was laying it on pretty thick, and if Jojo didn't have a massive ego, he might have been suspicious. But as it was, he let a smile creep over his face.

"You're just saying that," he said.

"There's a reason someone put you in charge of the Boons," I said. "You have an ability to make everyone feel at ease. And even though you hide under fifty layers of humor and sarcasm, it's obvious you genuinely care about all of us."

It sounded like I was still complimenting him to lead him away from the truth, but as I said the words, I realized how true they were. Jojo was a genuinely good person. He was a lot. That was for sure. But there wasn't anyone else I'd want in my corner if things got rough.

"Are you angling for a promotion?" he asked me, his eyes narrowed. "I know I'm great and all, but this seems too nice of you. 90s kids aren't known for being grandiose in their appreciation of amazingness."

"Are you kidding?" I asked. "90s kids invented being overzealous in their adoration. Have you seen Backstreet Boys fangirls?"

"No, and I hope I never do."

I laughed. "That's a fair point. But I'm serious, you're easy to be friends with, and I think Jenny likes hanging out with you. That's all."

Jojo nodded, puckering his lips as he did so.

"Are you not allowed to date Boons?" I asked. "Would what's-his-name in HR have a fit about it?"

"That idiot?" Jojo asked. "No. But it is a little frowned upon thanks to those drama queens in the Guardian department. Apparently, jealous exes have a tendency to turn into Beguilers. Plus, I'm still hoping to connect with Vesper."

"Yeah, how is that going?"

Jojo made a sound like a walrus groaning, his eyes dramatically aimed at the ceiling. "Apparently she's got some new boyfriend, so I'll have to wait for him to die, I guess."

"Jojo!"

"What? Everybody dies, kid. And it's not like I'm going to kill him. I'm just playing a waiting game."

I shook my head. "All right, well, your terrible dating advice aside, did you find anything out about Father Hawthorne?"

"You mean the hot priest?" Jojo corrected.

"Yes, the hot priest. Although I don't know if I love calling him that if he had something to do with my death."

"You can be hot and still be a bad person," Jojo pointed out. "In fact, the two go together a lot more often than you'd think."

"Jojo, focus," I said, snapping my fingers in front of his face like he was a dog I was training. "What did you find?"

"I talked to Seraph, and he said this guy isn't a Guardian or a Beguiler, which means he's not in our afterlife."

I pursed my lips at this. He wasn't in our afterlife?

"So, he's… in the next stage?" I asked. "Or he's still alive."

"I have absolutely no idea," Jojo admitted. "Which is rare for me. I normally know everything."

"Except if my death was an accident or a homicide."

"Calm down, I've got more information. It's not about the hot priest per se," he began. "I have a hacker connection who looked into this for me."

"A hacker connection?" I repeated skeptically. "Who's hacking for you? Can you even hack in the afterlife?"

"Oh, he's not dead. He's a technopath," Jojo said, as if this word should make sense to me. When I gave him a blank stare, he continued. "Someone who's connected to technology on a psychic level. Plus, I manifested to him, so he doesn't actually know I'm the boss of the afterlife."

"Why do you get to break the rules all the time, but I can't?"

"Because I'm in charge. It's one of the many perks. That and getting higher pay."

"I don't get paid," I said.

"Exactly," Jojo answered with a smug grin before continuing. "So, I had him track down the identity of the person who was supposed to meet you for your hot date the night you died."

"Oh good. You know about that, too," I said, placing my face in my hands. "Because it wasn't embarrassing enough to tell William about being stood up and then dying."

Jojo shrugged his shoulders. "You know you can't keep secrets from me for long. Besides, you'll want to hear what I found."

"Spill it," I said.

"The guy you spoke to online was listed as John Doe, but he did have a profile picture."

"I remember that," I said with a nod. "I don't really remember what he looked like in the picture, but everyone had profile pictures back then. And the fact that he looked male and sort of attractive was apparently enough for me."

"So, I got the picture from my friend," Jojo began slowly. "Since webcams in the 90s were basically potatoes, it's difficult to see much, but this looks an awful lot like the hot priest to me."

Jojo handed over the picture his "hacker friend" had given him, and I squinted at it.

He was right. It was incredibly blurry. I was sure that back in the 90s I would have looked at that and thought it was crystal clear, but even as a ghost, I'd been spoiled by technological advancements. When I was still alive, I'd thought the snake game on my Nokia was the epitome of mobile gaming.

How little I knew.

"It does look a lot like him," I said, studying the black hair, dark eyes, and pale skin. "He's just missing the nametag that says 'hot priest'."

"A nametag I need to start wearing," Jojo said, just as I heard the front door of the house open.

There was only one person who used the front door: Brody.

Brody was here. And Jojo was here. And I was about to be in so much trouble if Jojo saw him.

"You know what?" I said loudly, trying to drown out any sound Brody might make.

I was sure that at any minute, he'd start calling out for me.

"I'm not positive this is the hot priest. Can you go find Jenny and ask her what she thinks?" I was trying to keep my cool but doing an awful job of it. I had to hope Jojo wouldn't notice. "This seems like a really big clue, and I think we should figure it out right away."

"Sounds like a plan, boss. You lead the way." Jojo took my hand in his, waiting for me to pull us to Jenny, but I couldn't leave Brody in the house alone. What if William showed up again? I had to keep everyone away from each other, and I'd never been a great juggler.

"I think Jenny is at one of her haunts tonight," I said. "We should probably split up to find her faster." I took my hand out of Jojo's.

"Good thinking. I knew you were a smart one," he said with a grin. "I'll head to the Wille's if you want to check out the Parmley's."

"I'm on it," I said with a too-bright smile, watching as Jojo gave me a salute and disappeared. "Oh, thank goodness," I breathed.

"Jane?" Brody called.

Could that have possibly been any closer?

Chapter 20

I still hadn't mastered the art of manifesting to living people. Probably because it wasn't something we were supposed to do very often. It was reserved for special haunts and pre-approved visits to loved ones.

Still, I was getting faster at it the more I manifested to Brody. And he seemed to be getting more comfortable with a dead 90s kid suddenly appearing in front of him in an abandoned house.

"Jane!" Brody's face lit up when he saw me, and deep down, my fangirl heart still beat a little faster at the gesture. But it wasn't quite as exciting as it had been a few days ago.

Now it just made me miss William.

"I'm so glad you're here," he said, stepping forward, so we were closer together.

"I don't have the most buzzing social life now that I'm dead," I joked, even though the opposite had been true lately. "What are you doing here?"

Brody shuffled at my words, as if he felt awkward about his answer. "I was wondering if you managed to learn anything else about that thinner plane you told me about."

I had to rack my brain to figure out exactly what he was talking about. So much had happened since I'd talked to Brody. I'd found out that my death was a lot less cut-and-dry than I'd thought, and that revelation had taken up most of my brain power.

"You said there was a place where you could hear into the after-afterlife," he continued, watching me and waiting for my memory to catch up.

"Oh, right!" I exclaimed. "Sorry, I've had my hands full lately."

Brody smiled as he patiently waited for my braindead moment to pass.

"I found this place where I can hear something like whispers."

"Whispers?" he asked.

"From the next stage of the afterlife."

Brody nodded slowly. "That sounds pretty creepy."

I shivered at his words. "It was, actually."

He watched me for a moment as if he was waiting for me to talk. When I didn't, he went on. "I don't want to go all paranormal nerd on you, but last time you said you'd take me there so I could investigate." He paused, his eyes wide and hopeful. "Does that offer still stand?"

Did my offer still stand? Just because my crush on Brody had sort of evaporated in the face of William's awkward British-ness and amazing kisses, did that mean I could go back on my word? After all, this was Brody's livelihood. He loved studying the paranormal. And what was the harm in letting him bring his gadgets to the bamboo forest to see if he picked anything up?

That was a dumb question. I knew what the harm was. William trusted me. He trusted me with our spot. And here I was, bringing Brody there.

"Is something wrong?" Brody asked, seeing my hesitation.

"Well..." I wasn't quite sure what to say. I really didn't want to bring him there. But I was also a notorious people-pleaser.

"I know you said you're not really supposed to, but this could be the biggest breakthrough paranormal investigation has seen in a long time," he said, his voice full of hope. "You could be part of that. You could leave such a huge mark on this world."

My heart tightened in my chest. That did sound amazing. I did want to be known for more than just dying before I could return my movie to Blockbuster. And I didn't want to let Brody down, despite the fact that it felt icky to bring him to the spot that I'd kissed William.

Why was this such a hard decision?

"Please, Jane?" Brody pleaded.

I sighed. One last trip and then I'd cut ties with Brody.

"Okay," I relented. "I can bring you there,"

"You are an absolute angel!" Brody exclaimed.

"I do what I can," I said, forcing a smile even as I sat in the discomfort of my decision. "You'll have to meet me there, though. I can't exactly make you appear. Although that would have been rad if I could."

"So rad," he repeated with a grin.

"Are you mocking me?" I asked, my voice full of indignation. "Because I refuse to be mocked by a generation that came up with lame words like 'Yeet'."

"Technically, that's probably a generation younger than me," he said. "But point taken. You're too dope for that."

His eyes glinted as his grin widened. It almost made me forget about this immense betrayal of William's trust.

"Don't make me bust out 'da bomb' on you. Because so help me, I will," I said, smiling as I held up an "L" on my forehead.

"Burn," he said. "So where am I meeting you and when?"

"Oh right, we were actually discussing something professional," I answered. "Have you ever heard of The Huntington Library, Art Museum, and Botanical Gardens?"

"I think people usually call it The Huntington, but yes, I have," he said with a laugh.

"Okay, well, excuse me for trying to make sure you go to the right place." I grinned. "At The Huntington there's a bamboo forest." I paused. "How do you feel about breaking and entering? Because you'll probably want to meet me there after it closes."

Brody raised his eyebrows. "I'm not sure if breaking and

entering is the best option. Maybe I'll get a ticket to the gardens and hide out in a bathroom or something. That seems slightly less illegal for some reason."

"Rule follower," I taunted.

"I want to learn more about the paranormal, not go to jail," he answered with a shake of his head. "What time will you be there?"

"I'll meet you there tomorrow at seven," I said. "It closes at five, so that should give the staff enough time to close up shop and get out."

"That sounds perfect," Brody answered, smiling at me once more. "I don't think you realize how much I appreciate this. I know I get stupidly excited about paranormal stuff, but this really could be a breakthrough. If I can try out some of my technology to contact to the after-afterlife, that would be such a game changer."

I returned his smile. "Glad I could help."

Was I glad I could help? Not really. But I was doing it, anyway.

"I wish I could hug you or something," he said, his voice now shy.

I wanted to be excited by his words. And the idea of hugging a celebrity was still pretty awesome, but the idea of hugging Brody specifically didn't make my heart race like the idea of hugging William.

"Sorry," I stated simply. "Ghost."

"I guess I can't fix everything." Brody shrugged. "I'll see you tomorrow at the bamboo forest. Seven o'clock."

"I'll see you there."

***

To pass the time leading up to my meeting with Brody, I decided to do my job for the first time in a while. Even when I'd been haunting lately, I wasn't putting my whole heart into it. And so, I stood in the bedroom of a teenage girl on my list of approved families, wondering what kind of haunt I should go for.

"I feel a bit rusty," I said to the empty room. "Maybe just a moved paper for now."

Clearing my throat and stretching out my arm, I reached for a piece of paper on the girl's dresser and moved it a few inches.

The teenage girl, who was lying on her bed and texting, looked over at the paper for a moment before returning her gaze to her phone.

"Huh," I said, feeling like that wasn't quite the reaction I was hoping for. "I feel like I used to be better at this. Okay, round two."

This time, I moved the paper several more inches.

The girl glanced at the paper once more, pursed her lips, and went back to her phone.

"Seriously, kid? I'm giving you some great material here," I said. "Record it on your phone or something. Send it to a friend. Give me something."

"Not having a great night?" Jojo asked.

I didn't even jump at his presence this time. I was getting more and more used to Jojo appearing beside me.

"This girl is making me feel bad about myself," I whined.

"Chin up, kid. She's probably dealing with acne and pre-pubescent boys."

"Ew," I said, pulling a face. "You're right. She wins. I am *so* glad I don't have to deal with teenage boys anymore."

"That's the spirit," Jojo said with a smile.

I looked over at him and my smile instantly fell. "Jojo, what in the world are you wearing?"

He seemed to be incredibly proud of the pink short-sleeved collared shirt covered in pineapples with matching shorts. "Oh, this old thing? Had it for ages."

"It's... it's like one of those adorable baby outfits you buy where the pattern on the shirt matches the shorts but... you're a grown man."

"A grown man who's incredible enough to pull this off," he

said, gesturing widely to himself.

I nodded slowly. "Whatever you say, boss."

He narrowed his eyes at me. "Dear Jane, I think you're forgetting why you're here."

"Oh, I know why *I'm* here. I don't know why *you're* here."

"Right! I had a reason," he said, as if suddenly remembering. "Jenny thinks the random internet stalker looks like the hot priest, too. So, I think we have ourselves a good old-fashioned murder on our hands."

Jojo clapped his hands together, his expression gleeful.

"Jojo, could you refrain from looking so excited about the fact that I was killed by a priest?"

"A hot priest," he corrected.

"A hot priest," I agreed.

"Don't worry, sunshine, we'll figure it out." Jojo slapped me on the back. "But since I'm here, I'd love to see you in action. Consider it a quarterly performance review."

I groaned. "No way. This girl is lame. She doesn't care about my usual tricks."

Jojo gave me shook his head slowly at me, making me feel five years old again. "Now young lady, I want you to put on a can-do attitude right this instant and scare that poor teenager to death."

I rolled my eyes as dramatically as I could, but Jojo was unfazed. "Fine," I said, dragging the word out so that it was several syllables long.

Focusing, I pushed the piece of paper about a foot across the girl's dresser. Just like before, she glanced at it and then glanced back at her phone.

"Jojo," I said, my voice whiney again. "This is humiliating."

"Yeah, this little punk doesn't know who she's dealing with," he agreed. "Manifest to her!"

He sounded like a kid egging on a fight at school, but I obliged, making myself appear in the girl's room.

She looked up from her phone and let her eyes take me in from head to foot.

And then, I kid you not, she rolled her eyes.

I let my mouth fall open in shock. "Seriously? Did you just roll your eyes at me?"

"Are you supposed to be scary?" the girl asked. "The only thing scary about you is that sunflower dress."

"Oh burn!" Jojo said with a laugh, though the girl couldn't hear him.

"Shut up, Jojo," I said.

"My name's not Jojo," the girl answered.

"Yeah, I know it's not," I snapped back. "I wasn't talking to you, okay? The world doesn't revolve around you and your stupid phone."

"Whoa, Jane. Dial it back a bit. You're supposed to scare her, not lecture her."

"Ugh, I'm sorry, she's being really rude," I said. "It's throwing me off my game."

"Who are you even talking to?" the girl asked, her voice sounding like I was being a massive inconvenience to her.

"My super scary ghost friend. So, you'd better not make me mad or else I'll call him over," I said, trying to sound intimidating and failing miserably.

"I am so glad I stuck around for this." Jojo laughed, looking like he was enjoying my failure way too much.

"Look, I'm kind of busy, so could you like… leave?" the girl asked.

This was not going at all the way it was supposed to.

"Are you seriously not scared of me?" I asked.

She shook her head. "I like your sweet choker, though."

I may have appreciated the compliment, but I wasn't going to give her the satisfaction of a "thanks." She was being a bully.

"Listen, just because you've got TikTok to distract you doesn't mean you can be rude," I said.

"TikTok?" the girl asked, now openly laughing at me. "How old are you?"

"This just gets better and better," Jojo said, his eyes alight with joy.

"You know what?" I began, pointing a finger at the girl. "You need to learn to respect your elders."

"Oh, Jane. Stop while you're ahead." Jojo was practically in tears now.

Elders? I'd told her to respect her elders? I'd called myself an elder?

I needed to leave. This was quickly devolving into madness.

"Listen, I see way scarier stuff than this online every day. So thanks for trying to like… single me out with your weird ghost stuff, but I'm good."

I couldn't see my reflection in the girl's mirror, but I was pretty sure I looked completely stunned.

"I'm not a door-to-door missionary or something. I'm… I'm a ghost. How are you not shocked at all by this?"

The girl shrugged.

"Okay, well, this has been sufficiently humiliating. Please excuse me while I go find something else to do with my afterlife."

"Go full-haunt mode on her!" Jojo said, still sounding like he was egging on a fight. "Do it! She'll have to respect you then."

I sighed. "I'm so not in the mood," I told him before making myself disappear for the girl while still standing in the room.

"Bunch of weirdos," she said before looking back at her phone.

"Seriously?" I asked, now angry. "I'm going to pull her off of that bed and toss her out the window," I said, walking toward the girl before Jojo grabbed my arm and pulled me back.

"Easy there, tiger," he said, wiping a stray tear from his cheek. "Go cool off somewhere. You'll get her next time, I'm sure."

"I don't need your pity," I said, trying to keep my face angry even though I was feeling more embarrassed than anything.

"But you can have it anyway," Jojo said with a wink. "Seriously, go to the beach or something. I'll make sure I give this girl a good scare for you."

"You will?" I asked, starting to feel better.

"Anything for you, champ," he said, giving my arm a soft little punch.

"Thanks, Jojo."

I gave him a smile before pulling myself from the room and into the bamboo forest where I'd be meeting Brody that night.

"Jane?" William said, standing a few feet away on the path. "What are you doing here?"

Chapter 21

"William!" I said, smiling and instantly forgetting why I was there.

I walked over to him but paused just short of hugging him. Was I allowed to hug him? Were we there?

"What are you doing here?" I asked, even though he'd asked me first.

He smiled down at me, looking like he wanted to hug me just as much as I wanted him to.

"You were so interested in this spot the other day that I figured I'd try to investigate a bit," he said, biting his lip for a moment before continuing. "Plus, I now have quite good memories of this spot."

My long-dead heart felt like it stopped beating for a moment at his words. Had he just brought up our kiss unprompted? That had to mean he'd been thinking about it too, right?

I suddenly found myself staring at his lips, even though I tried not to.

"Yeah. Good memories," I said, my voice distant.

I had to focus. I couldn't get distracted by William's perfect smile or the dorky way he tried to be so proper around me when I could tell all we wanted to do was kiss each other.

Brody would be here soon, and I needed to get rid of William. But I wasn't quite sure how to do that.

"I'll be completely honest," William said, looking embarrassed. "I was hoping to make some sort of breakthrough as to why we can hear the whispers here, so I could impress you."

How could he be any more perfect?

I smiled up at him. "You wanted to impress me?"

He gave me a look like that should be obvious. "I always want to impress you," he said with a soft laugh. "It's a bit pathetic, if I'm honest."

I shook my head. "It's not pathetic," I said as I stood up on my toes and pressed my lips against his.

He immediately placed his hands on my waist to pull me against him, and my entire body felt like it was going to burst into flames. His fingers trailed around to my back and up into my hair as I deepened the kiss.

I loved the way I felt when I was with him.

It was like being alive again.

My chest moved against him as I breathed, inhaling and exhaling rhythmically together. I kissed him deeper then, wanting to relish in the feeling of being this close to him again. I wasn't sure it was ever something I'd take for granted.

I grabbed a handful of his coat to keep him close to me as his lips continued to move over mine. For someone who had almost no experience with kissing, he'd been a fast learner. I never wanted to stop kissing him. It was the most perfect feeling in the world. I would be fine spending eternity like this.

"I've missed you," he breathed against my lips.

"It's only been, like, a day," I said with a smile, pressing my forehead to his and leaning into him. "But I've missed you, too."

"I'm not a casually interested suitor," he went on, our noses touching. He placed a kiss against my lips, lingering there for a moment before pulling away just enough to speak. "I lied about that. I didn't want to scare you away."

It sort of felt like my heart was going to burst, but I managed to keep myself under control. "I'm not casually interested either," I confessed. "I'm all in."

His smile covered his entire face. "I completely adore you. Is that okay?"

"More than okay," I answered with a quick kiss. "I completely adore you, too."

The wide smile vanished and instead he kissed me again, more forcefully this time, as if he was no longer holding back. The passion in his kiss would have knocked me off of my feet if he hadn't been holding me tightly against him. Instead, I let myself melt into him and into the kiss.

After a moment, I let my lips trail to his sharp cheekbones, down to his jaw, down his neck, and to his collarbone. He let out a soft sigh as his hands tightened on my back. But a second later, his entire body tensed. I didn't have to see his face to know something was wrong.

"What's wrong?" I asked, looking behind me to see Brody walking down the path, completely unaware that William and I were standing there.

He passed by us, looking around the bamboo forest as if studying it.

"The Huntington is closed," William said, his voice low. "Why is Brody Specter here?"

My voice caught in my throat as I tried to think of any possible excuse that wouldn't make this look quite so bad.

William released me and took a step back, but I grabbed his hand before he could disappear without me.

"I know this looks bad," I began, my voice shaking as I watched the unbridled anger that flared behind his icy blue eyes.

"Why is Brody Specter here?" he asked again, his voice even deeper than usual.

If anger was the only emotion on William's face, I could have told myself he was being primitive and jealous, but the intense hurt that was hiding in his eyes almost broke my heart.

"Jane, please just tell me why he's here. I know it can't be as bad as I'm thinking," he said, now grasping for any excuse to trust me. "He's not meeting you here, right? It's just a coincidence?"

I pressed my lips together, my brow furrowed. The expression was apparently enough to confirm William's worst fears.

In an instant, he pulled his hand harshly away from mine and disappeared.

"William?" I called, even though I knew he was already gone.

I pressed my eyes together, trying to ignore the burning tears that wanted to fall.

I knew I shouldn't have kept meeting with Brody. Even if it wasn't romantic for me. I knew William would be hurt if he knew. I could have at least kept him in the loop, so it didn't seem so sneaky.

But here I was. Alone in the stupid bamboo forest. I couldn't even go after William because I had no idea where he'd gone.

Was he going to tell Jojo?

Something told me he wasn't. He was too hurt for that. Telling Jojo would be admitting how invested in me he was, and I didn't think William was quite ready to be that vulnerable with Jojo.

"This has to be it," I said to myself. "I'm going to show Brody where I heard the whispers, and then I'm going to tell him I can't talk to him anymore. It's not worth it."

William didn't trust Brody. He wanted to keep me safe. This went beyond William being possessive of me. He was far too polite to try to control me. But *I* didn't want to see Brody anymore. I didn't want to betray William's trust.

This was important to me. Because William was important to me.

This would be the last time I saw Brody Specter. And I'd have to hope after I helped Brody out, William would be able to look past the fact that I'd lied to him and trust me again.

Chapter 22

I manifested to Brody on the walkway in the bamboo forest, feeling like I wanted to be literally anywhere else at that moment.

Only seconds ago, this had been the spot of my absolute best memories in the afterlife, and now it felt forever tainted.

"There you are," Brody said. "I was starting to worry you were standing me up."

He walked over to me with a small black box in his hand before frowning.

"Are you okay? You look a little… tired. Can ghosts even get tired?"

"I'm fine," I said, my voice unsteady. "Listen… I can help you with this tonight, but after this, I can't really see you anymore."

Brody's eyebrows shot up. "Did that Jojo guy get you in trouble?"

I shook my head, wanting to get this whole thing over with so I could apologize to William and hopefully get back to my new normal with him. "I'm breaking the rules by seeing you, and it's hurting the people I care about."

"Hurting them?" he asked.

I could see why he was confused by my words. I wasn't exactly making much sense if he didn't know what was going on.

"The specifics aren't important, okay?" I asked, sounding a bit harsher than I meant to. "Sorry. This has to be the last time I see you."

Brody knitted his brows. "I can't say I'm not disappointed," he began. "Being a paranormal investigator, it's not often I get to see a full-bodied apparition, let alone talk to one. This has been life changing. *You've* been life changing."

His words should have flattered me. The old me would have melted into a puddle then and there. But all I could think about at the moment was where William could have possibly gone and how I could ever make this up to him.

At my silence, Brody went on. "Of course, I'll respect whatever you want," he said. "It's hard to let go of you already. I feel like we're connected or something."

I took a deep breath, not wanting to return his sentiments, but not wanting to be rude. "Should I show you where the spot is?"

Brody frowned. "Yeah. Okay."

I led him past the rail that separated the bamboo forest from the walking path. We weaved in between the tall, creaky bamboo until we came to a stop by the circular, scorched earth.

"Listen, Jane... if I've done something to offend you, I'm really sorry," Brody said.

"It really isn't you," I lied. "I'm not focusing on my job the way I should because of our meetings. I'm sorry if I sounded harsh before. I'm just... tired."

Tired. The catch-all word for "I don't want to talk about it."

Brody nodded again. "That's fine."

He looked at the black circle in front of the two of us and then to the box in his hands.

"What's that?" I asked, trying to change the subject to anything other than my illegal meetings with Brody.

"This is supposed to be a sort of spirit box," he explained.

"Spirit boxes don't work," I said automatically.

Brody cocked his head to the side. "You communicated with

me through a spirit box," he said. "That was how I knew where to find you in Ramona."

"Oh right," I said. "Sorry. Old habit. I've always thought spirit boxes were totally bogus. But I guess you're right."

I actually managed a smile for the first time since William had disappeared.

"This one is different from those electronic ones that use the radio," Brody said, looking down at the heavy black box.

"How does it work?"

"I'm not sure it even does," Brody said. "I bought it from someone who swears it belonged to Ed and Lorrain Warren. But who knows if he was telling the truth."

"That would be awesome if it did," I said with a smile. "I'm a big fan."

"Aren't we all?" Brody asked. "They're the best in the business."

"Present company excluded?"

"Obviously." Brody laughed before turning his attention back to the box. "This thing is hollow on the inside and has this circle cut out of the side." He put his mouth up to the circle and spoke. "So, it's really echo-y."

I managed a small smile as his voice echoed through the box. "Are you saying this is the original spirit box? Before all that radio nonsense?"

"Sort of. It's supposed to capture and amplify voices from beyond the grave." He made his voice overly dramatic as he spoke the last few words.

"You think it'll amplify the voices from the after-afterlife?"

"That's what I'm hoping. I'm not sure it'll actually work, but I figured there's no harm in trying. The worst thing that can happen is I've wasted an evening."

The worst thing was I'd lose William forever. But I didn't think Brody needed to know that.

"Let's try it out then," I said, forcing a smile.

"Perfect," he answered. "I'm going to set the box beside the dark circle. Would you mind standing inside? I need you to tell me if you're hearing them, so we can see if it translates through the box."

"Sure thing," I answered, taking my place in the burned area. "I can already hear them, can you not?"

"Nothing," Brody answered with a sad shake of his head. "But I need to activate the spirit box first, so that might be why."

"Activate it?" I asked.

"I know it sounds dumb, and it very well might be. But these are the instructions I was given," Brody said with a shrug.

He placed the box on the ground beside me before pulling a small object out of his pocket. He put it on top of the box, and I strained to see what it was.

It looked like a ring.

"Is this all part of the activation?" I teased, my smile faltering as I started to feel warm.

Warm? I never felt warm. I was a ghost. Ghosts were definitely not warm.

"Wait... can you hear them now? I think it might be working. I feel... weird," I said.

I couldn't actually hear the voices anymore, but my breathing suddenly picked up speed as my heart raced.

"I actually feel... sort of awful," I said, kneeling on the ground in the scorched circle beside the spirit box.

"Do you?" Brody asked, sounding completely unconcerned.

"Yeah it's... it's weird. I can't hear the voices. I just... I don't know. It's like a low blood sugar attack or something."

I swallowed hard, my chest feeling tight as my arms shook. The urge to close my eyes and go to sleep was overwhelming.

"Brody, I think your spirit box is defective," I said, my voice sounding weak. "We might need to put it away... it's..." my words trailed off as I looked at the black wooden box in front of me.

On top of it was a small plastic smiley face ring.

My smiley face ring.

The one I was currently wearing.

I looked down at my hand. It was still there. Of course, that was just the afterlife version of my ring. The actual ring had probably burned with my body, hadn't it?

I blinked several times, trying to fight the exhaustion overwhelming me. Leaning closer to the ring, I could see where the plastic was warped and bubbly.

This was my ring. My actual ring. This was the ring I'd been wearing when I'd died.

"Brody?" I asked, fear now beginning to line my words. "Where did you get that?"

Chapter 23

"This old thing?" he asked. "A friend sent it to me."

"A friend?" My mind grew fuzzy. "A friend sent you my ring?"

"Maybe 'friend' isn't the right word," Brody said. "More like a patron."

I furrowed my brow. "Brody, you're really starting to sound like you're evil-villain-monologing. Can you please explain what's going on?"

This actually made Brody laugh. Not a loud, booming, evil laugh. Just a soft one. That might have been creepier.

"I was contacted by a third party who's been researching the paranormal for years. At first, I thought they were just another fan, but it turns out, they really know their stuff."

This was definitely an evil villain monologue. But how could Brody possibly be bad? He had a reality TV show! TV had never betrayed me like this before. TV had raised me.

"I don't need the backstory," I said, my voice feeble. "Just tell me what in the world is happening."

"But the backstory is the best part of all this," he told me with a grin. "Don't you want to know why this box is so important?"

I did, but I didn't want to give him the satisfaction of knowing that. Although I really needed to know just how "evil"

Brody was. Was he just trying to get a picture of me with this box? Or was he trying to permanently kill me?

"Fine. Monologue away."

"Thank you," he said, sounding much too professional for how crappy I was feeling. "My contact hired me to utilize their research in my professional field. The first thing I had to do was make definitive contact with a spirit. Something beyond doubt." He stopped. "Like having some girl appear to me."

"That's me." I raised my hand before dropping it instantly, unable to keep it up.

"After I found you, I needed to ask about any locations where the veil between our two worlds seemed thinner. That was a major requirement for this box to work."

"And what does the box actually *do*?" I asked again, my patience growing thin. There was also the fact that it felt like I might pass out at any second. That wasn't exactly helping my patience.

Every muscle in my body seemed to shake, and I finally had to abandon my kneeling pose for lying on the ground.

"My contact has been researching different ways to bind spirits to objects." Brody went on, unphased by my increasingly pathetic state. "This box, for example, is supposed to be an old-fashioned spirit box. Theoretically, I should be able to bind you to this object."

"Great," I deadpanned.

"And based on your current state, I'd say it's definitely working." He narrowed his eyes. "Try to leave."

I scowled. This was the most bogus thing to happen to me. And I'd died in a house fire caused by a curling iron I hadn't even turned on.

"Sorry, but I'm kind of dealing with the fact that my celebrity ghost hunting idol is actual a giant buttface, so if you could give me a minute, that would be great." I managed to roll my eyes at Brody, even though it took monumental effort.

I always knew I'd die rolling my eyes. I didn't expect it to be a second death.

"I don't have time for this, Jane. Try to leave. I need to know if this is working."

I was too weak to stand up and try to leave, so I opted for rolling to my back and staring up at the creep.

"You know what, Brody? You're the worst. I trusted you. I've been your fan for years." I glared, wishing I'd never broken the rules to make contact with him. My stupid love of TV had gotten me into way too much trouble this time. "I used to think you were the best thing to happen to the paranormal field."

"And now?" he asked, sounding like he really didn't care but humoring me, anyway.

"You can eat my shorts."

It wasn't the best insult I'd ever come up with, but it would have to do in my current state.

"Now that you've gotten that out of your system, will you please try to leave?"

If I hadn't been so incredibly weak and tired, I would have been seething with rage. As it was, I was only sort of aware of how annoying this entire situation was.

I'd lost William's trust over someone who didn't care about the paranormal or me. He only cared about the way the paranormal could serve his career. None of this had been worth ruining my relationship with William and lying to Jojo.

"Move!" Brody finally yelled.

"Dude, I've been trying this whole time. Calm down, would you? Your stupid box worked." I would have been more scared about the implications of being "tied to an object" if I'd been in my right mind. But I was about two seconds from passing out. Was this karma for all the times I'd accidentally killed my virtual pet? Is this what Horson Welles had felt like every time I'd forgotten to feed him his hay?

"Perfect. So, it works."

"Congratulations."

"I've bound you to this spirit box. You have no choice… you're attached to it now."

"Like *Ghostbusters*."

"What?" he asked.

"You know... the movies?"

Brody gave me an unimpressed look. How had I not noticed what a jerk he was? Was I that starstruck? He'd been way too interested in Jojo and the afterlife. But I had to let my stupid celebrity crush get in the way of logic. As usual.

"Now that you're bound to this object, I don't have to listen to you drone on endlessly about your precious 90s pop culture. I can just shut you up."

"Shut me up?" That didn't sound pleasant.

Brody knelt beside me and smiled. It wasn't as cute as I remembered. Now it gave me a pit in my stomach.

"Goodnight, Jane."

Chapter 24

"You with the sad eyes."

I groaned at the familiar voice, even though I knew it meant I'd possibly been saved from a horrible nightmare. "Jojo. No Cyndi Lauper right now. I've had the worst night."

I opened my eyes to find myself in blackness. I wanted to call it a room, but it wasn't really a room. It was just... a space.

"Jojo?" My annoyed voice suddenly took on a worried quality. "Jojo where am I?" I sat up to see Jojo sitting cross-legged in front of me in his ridiculous pink pineapple outfit. It didn't seem like appropriate attire for the situation at hand.

"Shhh. Calm down my little Beanie Baby. We're going to figure this out," Jojo said, his voice adopting a soothing air.

It wasn't working.

"I'm freaking out. I don't know where I am. Where are we?"

Jojo winced. "All right. So, *we* technically aren't anywhere. I have no idea where you are. And I'm not even sure how I was able to, contact you since I'm not physically with you."

"You're not?" I reached out to touch Jojo, only to have my hand go straight through him. "Jojo, manifest to me. Right now. I need someone here. I don't know what's going on." My voice was in full-on panic mode, and I knew it. But I couldn't calm myself.

Brody's evil villain monologue hadn't been a bad dream. I

really was stuck somewhere in that stupid spirit box.

"Jane, I know this is scary, but you've got to calm down. I have no idea how stable our connection is, and if you freak out, it might shatter."

Jojo was being incredibly normal, and it scared me even more than his weirdness.

I tried to keep calm like he advised, but it was near impossible. I was confused and lost and scared.

"Jojo, I messed up. I mean *really* messed up. I totally ignored your rules, I lied to William, and I think I'm going to die again. What even happens to me if I die a second time?" Tears pooled in my eyes as I twisted my smiley face ring around and around.

"What exactly happened? It can't be all that bad. You probably accidentally slipped into a quantum dimension or something. It happens to the best of us."

I shook my head, feeling my cheeks warm as the realization hit me. I was going to have to tell Jojo everything.

"I've been lying to you. I've been meeting with Brody Specter and talking to him." Jojo watched me carefully but didn't seem particularly surprised by my revelation. "I told him a little about the afterlife and he... he just kept asking me more and more questions. I was stupid and thought he was interested professionally, but I think he had an ulterior motive."

I said "I think" to soften the blow. I knew he had ulterior motives.

"Why do you think that?" Jojo asked. "Besides the fact that he's a reality TV star."

"Brody said he wanted to research a place where the veil between our worlds was thin. I took him to the bamboo forest at The Huntington because I thought I'd found a spot there where I could hear whispers from the after-afterlife."

I paused, taking a shuddering breath as a few stray tears streaked down my cheeks. I wouldn't let myself sob. I had to be strong. But that didn't stop a few salty traitors from escaping.

"He had this old-timey spirit box and... did some kind of ritual. Somehow, he'd gotten my ring from another paranormal investigator, and he used it to bind me to the box. I guess he'd been researching how to control spirits or something."

Jojo nodded slowly, still looking entirely too casual in his pineapple outfit to be in charge of rescuing me.

"I'm not gonna lie to you, kid. That doesn't sound good. But no one takes my favorite Boon without my permission." Jojo looked over his shoulder as if someone might overhear him, even though we were alone in this black crushing void. "Don't tell anyone you're my favorite. It probably wouldn't sit well with the other thousands of Boons I'm over."

"Please tell me there's something you can do. I'm scared, Jojo."

For the first time in the twenty years I'd known him, Jojo's face melted from the easy smile into a mask of worry. His brows knitted as he watched me with his dark brown eyes. "I'm going to save you Jane. I promise. I don't know how. But I'll figure it out." He chewed his lip for a moment while he thought. "Is there any way you can try to manifest? That would help us locate you."

"Brody said he can control me now that I'm bound to the box. I couldn't even disappear when I tried. I don't think I'll be able to manifest unless he lets me."

"Well, he's going to have to let you eventually. Otherwise, what's the point of having you bound in the first place? He obviously wants to use you for something." Jojo tapped his thumb against his knee absently. "He'll make you manifest. And when he does, we'll come for you. I'll get William to help."

At the mention of William's name, my heart sank. "Jojo, I messed things up with him. I lied to him about Brody. I totally broke his trust."

"Jane, William is worried sick about you. Something tells me he's already forgiven you. Getting kidnapped by a psychopath was probably the best thing to happen to your relationship." Jojo managed to bring a ghost of his former smile to his face. "Besides, the whole reason I brought him over here from England was to set you two up. I'm not letting some dumb mistake ruin my grand plan."

"I knew it."

"Of course you did. Because you're brilliant. And also because I've already told you this a thousand times." Jojo's grin was in full force.

"Will you still tell him how sorry I am? I was stupid, and he deserved better than that."

"Anything for you two," Jojo said with a wink. "Now don't lose hope. As soon as Brooding Ghostface lets you manifest, we'll be all over that guy. He thinks he likes ghosts? He won't once we're done with him."

A small smile crossed my lips. "Thank you, Jojo. For everything. You're always here for me, and I feel like I don't tell you enough how much I appreciate it."

"Don't get all sappy on me yet. We'll have plenty of time for that when we find you."

"Yes sir," I said, giving him a little salute—our private little gesture I'd grown so accustomed to.

"At ease," he answered, reaching out to touch my hand before stopping. "Sorry… forgot I'm not really here with you. I'll see you soon, kid."

I nodded, even though my face betrayed just how worried I was that I'd never see him or William again. "Okay."

Jojo returned my little salute before disappearing.

As soon as he left, the tremendous fatigue washed over me. I wasn't sure if Jojo had somehow staved it off, or if I'd been able to ignore it while he was there. But I was suddenly overwhelmed by the urge to lie down and go to sleep.

I wasn't sure if I'd actually fallen asleep, but it seemed like time began to pass in a sort of fever dream. I'd wake every once in a while, not know how long I'd been out or if I'd actually woken up at all. There was no way for me to make any sense of what I was seeing around me when I woke.

After what felt like years and seconds all at once, the sensation of a hard surface pressed against my cheek.

I opened my eyes to find myself in a small space. But this

space was real. It wasn't some random swirling voice of blackness. Instead, it looked like I was in a wooden box.

"Oh no. I'm inside the stupid spirit box, aren't I?"

"Luckily, no," an unfamiliar voice said nearby.

I jumped slightly at the unexpected sound, looking around frantically. It only took me a minute to realize what I was seeing.

"Am I... in a confession booth?" I asked the voice behind the screen. "Does this mean I died again? Is this like the test to get into the after-afterlife?"

Had Jojo really not been able to save me? It only made sense that if I died a second time, I'd end up in a confession booth. Honestly, it made more sense than dying and waking up in some random Kiwi's living room. At least a confession booth sort of tracked with what I thought I'd known about the afterlife.

"Do you know what's going on, Jane?" the voice asked me.

I'd expected the final judgment to be in a massive room with scary-looking angels and a man with a white beard and a deep booming voice. But this guy had a surprisingly high voice. It wasn't necessarily girly. But it was... different. British, high-pitched, and unconcerned.

"I have no idea."

"Have you spoken to Jojo? Did he explain anything to you?"

I squinted at the screen separating the voice from me but couldn't make out who was on the other side. "No... I haven't spoken to Jojo in... a long time... I think."

"Ah, yes. Time might seem a bit odd right now. That's understandable." The voice paused before continuing. "So, Jojo's not with you, then? That's disappointing."

I shook my head. "Is he supposed to be? Is he allowed in this next part of the afterlife?"

Nothing was making sense, and the confession booth was starting to make me feel claustrophobic. I pushed on the wooden door, but it didn't open.

"Jojo's only in charge of—"

"The Boons," I finished, before stopping to consider what I'd just said. "Did you not already know that?"

Who was this guy? If he was the gatekeeper between the afterlife and the after-afterlife, shouldn't he know what Jojo's job was? And where Jojo was?

"Of course," the man said, as if he hadn't asked me for information that should be obvious. "And other than Boons, who have you encountered in the twenty years you've been dead?"

Red flags sprang to life in my mind. Maybe this guy wasn't the gatekeeper to the next stage of the afterlife. And if he wasn't, I definitely shouldn't be giving him information about Jojo and the other Boons.

"I don't feel comfortable telling you anything else until you tell me what's going on here," I said, still trying to make out who was on the other side of the confession booth screen.

The man sat in silence for a moment before I saw his form move out of the space.

"Fine. We can do this the hard way."

Chapter 25

I stood to leave the confession booth, but not because I wanted to. I could no longer control my body as my legs moved of their own accord.

"Are you kidding me right now?" I asked no one in particular.

I was getting really sick of being a meat puppet.

My hands pushed the door to the confession booth wide open as I fell out of it onto the stone floor of a beautiful old church. The gray stone walls and archways would have been an incredible sight to behold if I hadn't been more shocked by something else.

"The hot priest!" I yelled.

It wasn't my most eloquent moment.

The man in the priest collar standing in front of me let his lip quirk up into a sideways smile as he paced in front of me. He looked like he was tossing the name around in his head.

"Hot priest? Is that what the kids are calling me these days?" he asked.

He looked exactly like the picture the police had taken twenty years ago. The same black hair, pale skin, and black eyes. The same high cheekbones and harsh features. He hadn't aged a day.

That couldn't be a good thing.

William had mentioned "creatures" before… maybe the hot priest wasn't human?

"Don't get me wrong, I love the idea of being called Hot Priest. I wasn't expecting to be flattered right out of the confession booth. This is all moving so fast."

I stared at the man with an open mouth. I couldn't make sense of what I was seeing.

"You… you talked to the police after I died," I said, because it was the only thing I could think to say. "And you… dated Jenny." I pulled a face at this. "What the crap?"

Again, I wasn't winning any prizes for being eloquent.

"You know what, I'm going to start going by 'Hot Priest.' I think it suits me. I can even get little wax stamps with 'HP' on them," he said, as if he hadn't even heard me. "Although, then people may associate me with Harry Potter, and I can't have that. Copyright."

"Um… what's going on?" Was it possible that the hot priest was even harder to keep on track than Jojo? Because if so, I was in a world of trouble. "How could you possibly be there to talk to the police when I died?"

The hot priest turned his quirked smile in my direction, looking like he was incredibly excited to answer that question. "Dear Jane. I feel like I've really gotten to know you over these past few weeks. I'm so glad we live in the same area. Maybe we can meet? I'd love to finally see you face to face."

My stomach dropped. I tried to swallow but my mouth was bone dry.

"Sorry I never made it to our date," he said with a wince and a shrug. "I was too busy drugging your water. Plus, you know, first date jitters. I never know how to make small talk."

"You killed me? You… you drugged my drink?" I asked, horror lining my words.

"Either that or you're an incredibly sound sleeper," he said. "I'm not sure how else you could sleep through having your body burned to a crisp. Not even I have that much self-control." He pulled a face. "Let's be honest, I have no self-control."

"You're the reason I didn't wake up when the house burned down?"

"Guilty," he said with a gleeful little laugh. "I'm also the reason the house burned down in the first place. I was a busy man that night. So again, I apologize for missing our date. But I had a lot going on. We can always try again."

I was on my hands and knees, unable to fully stand while the hot priest apparently had me under his control.

"Why would you kill me?" I felt too vulnerable. I wanted William there. I wanted Jojo there. I wanted anyone with me who could tell me it would be okay.

"I mean, honestly, killing people is kind of my thing," he said in a nonchalant way. "Have you never tried it? Because it's incredibly addicting. Like crisps. You can't have just one." He pursed his lips together. "But with you I had an actual reason for it."

The hot priest knelt beside me and placed his hand under my chin, lifting my head so I had to look at him. His eyes searched my own, roaming over my face as the sadistic smile spread across his lips once more. He was terrifying.

"You look exactly the same as the day I killed you," he said. "Is that a thing? Do you have to wear whatever you died in? Because while I commend your dedication to 90s fashion, I would have thought you'd lose the sunflower dress by now."

I kept my eyes trained on his soulless dark eyes, even though I wanted to look away. "Afterlife rule," I said, keeping my voice unconcerned despite the crushing panic I was feeling.

I was channeling my inner Daria.

His hand was still on my chin, squeezing my jaw painfully between his thumb and pointer finger. "You're awfully pretty," he said, the smile growing.

"How can you touch me? I didn't manifest to you. And even if I had, the living can't normally feel the dead."

The hot priest made a tsk sound and shook his head, but never let my face go. "I made you manifest. We're in the living plane right now. And I'm not technically living, so I can touch you all I want. I can make you do *whatever I want.*" He drew out the last few words in a way that made me shiver, despite my best efforts to conceal how disturbing this man was.

If he'd made me manifest, it was only a matter of time before Jojo found me. He'd promised he'd find me. As soon as I manifested, he'd be looking.

Unless it had taken too long. I wasn't sure how much time had passed, but it felt like forever. What if Jojo had given up looking for me? What if he'd assumed I was lost forever?

"Who are you?" I asked, both because I wanted to know and also because I was stalling for time. I needed to give Jojo a fighting chance to find me.

The hot priest released my face and stood to his full height, forcing me to stand in the process.

"I suppose I haven't properly introduced myself, have I? Although I'm not sure I want to. Hot Priest is so much catchier."

He smiled a lot.

"Braham Hawthorne," he said, with a dramatic little bow. He then pulled a face. "The bow was too much, wasn't it? Was it too much? I like a bit of theatrics, but that might have crossed the line to kitschy."

"It felt stilted," I told him.

He nodded. "Yeah, I thought so, too."

"You said there was an actual reason you killed me?" I needed to keep him talking. "I feel like I have a right to know."

Braham rolled his eyes with an exasperated sigh. It put my signature eye roll to shame. "Ugh. Fine. You want me to evil villain monologue like Brody?"

"You mean your field agent?"

"He was boring. So serious about everything," Braham said. "I already killed him."

My eyes widened. "You killed Brody Specter? Why? When? He's famous! The cops are definitely going to come after you."

"Always the same questions. I would think a ghost would

offer something more to this discussion, but you're just like the rest of them." He sounded bored. "I killed Brody the second he brought me the spirit box," Braham began, holding up his fingers as if ticking off items on his to-do list. "What was the next one? Why, right?" I nodded, my face still frozen in an expression of horror. Brody was a tool, but it was still shocking to hear the hot priest talk about killing him in such a nonchalant way. "Because he was boring and average, just like everyone else. I'm so tired of boring people. I want someone extraordinary."

"Aren't you worried you'll get caught?"

"I've been doing this for over a hundred years and haven't been caught yet. I like my chances," he said.

So, he wasn't human.

"What are you?"

"Rude," he answered. "So rude. But a fair question."

Braham continued to walk around me in slow circles, picking at his nails as he did so. He seemed incredibly bored with me, but he was still talking, so that was something.

"I'm immortal. As far as I can tell. I used to be a priest back in the English countryside, and one day I just noticed I wasn't aging like I should be." He said all of this as if it were completely normal. "At first I was a bit nervous about the whole thing, but eventually I realized if I never die, I can do whatever I want."

"And so instead of curing cancer or ending world hunger, you chose to kill people?"

"Magnificent, isn't it? No one else is as special as me, which makes everyone my play things. It's brilliant."

"You're a sociopath," I said, my brows knitted together.

Braham laughed. "You're sweet. But a sociopath suggests remorse. I'm actually a psychopath." He pointed to his head before continuing. "Some psychologists think it's because of brain lesions that psychopaths lack remorse, but I think it's because we know how to have a good time."

He shrugged and continued circling me.

"How did you even go from being a priest to killing people? That seems like a jump."

"It's kind of a funny story, actually," he said, laughing again. The sound was chilling. "I had this woman in my Parrish in England I fancied. She was being courted by some dope, and he intended to propose. Now, technically speaking, I wasn't supposed to form any romantic attachments as a man of the cloth, but I made an exception for her."

My breath caught. There was no way this was going where I thought it was going. Right?

"I promised her a lavish life if she got rid of her suitor, and she obliged," he said. "It wasn't even difficult. The prat knocked himself out while trying to propose. All she had to do was let him drown."

Braham laughed again, but I felt like I might be sick.

He'd killed William. William had been Braham's first victim. That couldn't be a coincidence, could it?

"How did you convince her to do all this?" I asked, my words stilted as I tried to keep my composure, even though I wanted to vomit.

"Why do you think I became a priest?"

"Because you believe in God?" I asked, to which Braham scoffed.

"I'm good at convincing people of things. Amassing followers has always been something of a gift." He smiled again. "I thought, why not put that to good use?"

I watched him as he continued to pace. This was all too much. I needed to sit down, but I couldn't because he was forcing me to stand. "What happened to the girl?"

Braham gave me a look like this should be obvious. "Got bored. Got rid of her."

This man was an actual full-fledged psychopath. I'd only been with him for ten minutes, and I'd heard about at least three counts of first-degree murder. I normally wasn't scared for myself since I was already dead, but given the power this guy seemed to have, I was starting to worry there might actually be things worse than death.

"All this to say I have some level of control over people I've killed," he said. "At least, that's my working theory. I believe they're indebted to me. And if I can figure out how to really harness that, I can make myself an indestructible little band of followers." He grinned. "And how fantastic would that be?"

"But you needed the spirit box to control me," I pointed out. Why was I helping him?

"I needed the spirit box to wrangle you in, but I'm fairly certain I would have had some bit of control over you without it. This just sped things up."

I watched him carefully, reading his face as best I could. He didn't seem to actually know if he had control over me without the box. It was just a theory. And before Brody had used the box to trap me, Braham had never used me in any way. Maybe there was still hope in this increasingly hopeless situation.

"Let's test this out, shall we?" he asked as I fell to my knees.

An unseen force pushed my head down, posing me in a sort of bowing position. Braham hadn't even lifted a finger. He hadn't said some magic spell. He just thought about what he wanted me to do and I had to do it.

That implication was terrifying.

"Excellent," he said as he came to stand in front of me. All I could see were the toes of his polished black shoes, but his voice seemed closer than it should have been.

It only took me a moment to realize I was hearing his voice in my head.

"I own you now."

Chapter 26

I struggled against Braham's control, desperately wanting to look him in the eye so I'd sound more convincing, but had to settle for staring at the floor.

"You may think you own me, but Jojo will come for me, and you'll be sorry when he does."

At my words, Braham seemed to release me from his control long enough for me to stand. Of course, the second I made a move toward him, he froze me in place again.

"Ah yes. Jojo. He was the one I had Brody gather information on. He did a rubbish job. He was so obvious." Braham shook his head. "He was an incompetent tool, I'll admit. But he got what he deserved, so no harm done."

I tried to focus on the fact that Braham knew who Jojo was, rather than the fact that the man I'd had a celebrity crush on only a few days ago was now evil and dead.

"I'm very interested in Jojo. He isn't *the* one I'm interested in ultimately. That's another story for another day. But he's fascinated me for some time."

"How do you even know about Jojo?" I asked.

"Your idiot friend Jenny told me a lot," he said. "Honestly, I thought it would be hard to convince someone in the afterlife I was dead, but she was surprisingly easy to mold." At this, he let his eyes roam slowly over me. "You, I suspect, would be more difficult to fool. You're smarter."

"How did you even talk to her? You can't force her to manifest. She's not under your control."

"Being in the unique position I'm in, I can commune with the afterlife. To some extent. And, as I said, I didn't have to work hard to convince her I was dead. She didn't really ask many questions."

Braham watched me, his eyes still taking me in uncomfortably. He took a step toward me and ran his fingers through my hair. I tried to step away but couldn't.

"Oh, how I wish I'd killed Jojo," he said, sounding like someone who regretted not purchasing concert tickets.

His fingers continued to comb my hair before they encircled my throat for the briefest of moments.

"I'd love to have control of the man who controls the Boons. But Jojo was before my time." He brought his hand to my cheek and softly traced my cheek bone, staring at my lips as he did so. "I'll have to settle for controlling his favorite instead. That's almost the same as controlling him."

I swallowed hard, my jaw tight as I spoke. "I'm not Jojo's favorite."

Braham laughed, the sound loud with how close he was. "Jojo is so human for someone who's supposed to be above it all. He's so emotional and needy. It took me five seconds of talking to Jenny to figure out you were his favorite. The fact that I'd finally managed to kill someone Jojo would bond with was a relief. I was beginning to worry I was picking terrible candidates." Braham kept his hand on my cheek. "I should have known he'd be so predictable."

He leaned in closer to me now.

"A sarcastic 90s kid with a pop culture obsession. It shouldn't have taken me so long to figure that out. But all good things take time."

"Jane," I heard a voice say, so close to me I almost jumped.

I couldn't turn my head to see who it was, but I'd know that impossibly deep voice anywhere. It was William.

He was right next to me.

And Braham had no idea.

"Get your hands off her," William said.

"He can't hear you, mate," Jojo said, also sounding incredibly close.

No one seemed to understand personal space today.

"I'll make him hear me," William said, his voice low and terrifying.

"No!" I said, before realizing I might be giving them away.

"Jane's right. Stay hidden. You're more useful to us that way." Jojo walked forward to get a better look at Braham before letting out a low whistle. "Jenny's right. He is hot. I can't even blame her for giving away the secrets of the afterlife."

"No, what?" Braham said, smiling at the thought he was finally getting to me. He leaned closer. "What's wrong?"

"I know you think you're smart, but I'm not Jojo's favorite," I said, hoping my save was at least somewhat believable.

"You are, actually," Jojo said, quite unhelpfully. Thank goodness Braham couldn't see him or hear him. Jojo had no poker face. "No offense, William. You're my second favorite. But Jane will always be my BFF."

"So, you being able to control my body won't get you anywhere, because Jojo doesn't care about me," I said.

I was desperately trying to fill Jojo and William in on a few things without letting Braham know they were there. I wasn't sure if they knew Braham was controlling me right at that moment, but a few context clues should help.

"How can he control her?" William asked, now coming to stand in front of me, right beside Braham.

I wanted to smile when I saw his face. His icy blue eyes were filled with concern, and a hard line formed between his brows as he looked at me.

Even in the current circumstance, seeing William in front of me was like a wave of relief.

Braham dropped his hand from my cheek and took a step back as if to size me up again, and I'd never been so happy to have distance from someone.

"You think I'm daft, and it's insulting," he said. "I'm not like you. I'm not ordinary. Your little lies don't work with me. If I control Jojo, even by proxy, I control a significant portion of the afterlife."

"I always knew my magnetic personality would bring about the apocalypse one day," Jojo said with a sad shake of his head.

I wanted to scold him for being so flippant, but I couldn't without giving him away to Braham.

Part of me thought that was why he was doing it—he knew I couldn't scold him right now.

"Is the spirit box the only thing keeping me tethered to you?" I asked, mostly to let the boys know why I was stuck in this situation.

Braham gave me a look like I was a complete idiot. "I already told you that by killing you, I gained a certain level of control," he said.

"He what?" William asked, his eyes darting from mine over to Braham. Somehow, his light blue eyes seemed to go dark at Braham's words.

"Mate, this isn't the time to defend your girlfriend's honor," Jojo said. "First, we've got to save her."

"Jojo, he killed her," William said, his entire face contorting into a mask of pure rage.

"And if he hadn't, you wouldn't have a girlfriend right now," Jojo said, like someone trying to talk a person off of a ledge. "Look at the silver lining. He sort of did you a favor."

I knew William wasn't buying Jojo's logic at all, but I was hoping it would be enough to calm him down. I needed him out of sight so he could fix this for me.

"So, if the spirit box was destroyed, you'd lose some power over me?" I asked.

My questions were too pointed, and I knew it. I was just counting on Braham's massive ego to keep him talking.

He was clever, and he wanted everyone to know it.

Braham watched me with narrowed eyes for a moment

before his entire face lit up.

"Jojo! I feel honored that you'd grace me with your presence," Braham said, even though Jojo hadn't manifested yet.

"Okay, that's creepy," Jojo said. "He's a witch!"

"He's not a witch," I said, knowing Jojo's cover had already been blown. "He's just clever."

"Oh stop," Braham said with mock modesty, before looking around the old abandoned church. "So, do I get to see you face to face, or are you going to keep hiding from me?"

"William, I'm going to need you to find a way to destroy that spirit box," Jojo said quickly, giving William instructions while he still could. "I don't care what rules you have to break or who you have to show yourself to. We need that thing gone to get Jane away from the hot priest."

William kept his eyes locked on Braham for a moment longer before finally nodding. "I can do that. Just buy me some time to find it."

"Anything for you," Jojo said before slapping William on the butt.

My eyes widened, and I would have laughed, had it not been something of a death or permadeath situation.

Without another word, William disappeared from the room.

A moment later, Jojo manifested, standing right in front of Braham.

Chapter 27

Braham's face lit up with a wide and unnatural grin that didn't reach his eyes. "Jojo."

Jojo gave a courtesy nod before saying, "Hot Priest."

"Please, my friends call me Braham," he said, extending his hand. Jojo took it briefly.

The entire exchange was incredibly awkward.

Of course, it didn't help matters that Jojo was wearing his pink shorts and matching collared shirt with pineapples all over them. He didn't exactly cut an intimidating figure.

Not like an imposing man in a priest collar.

We really needed to appoint an afterlife uniform committee. You couldn't look like an intimidating man with your knees showing. It was a fact.

"This is a fun little setup you've got here, Father," Jojo said, looking around the abandoned church with an impressed nod. "I'd probably put a few bean bag chairs near the old pulpit, but other than that, it's not bad. Just a bit drafty."

Braham looked Jojo over, taking in the pineapple shorts and white sneakers. "Not that I'm ever one to knock self-expression in all its forms, but... I thought you'd be a bit more... impressive."

"And I thought a raging sociopath would be more impressive, but here we are," Jojo said, never once breaking his stride as he circled the room, checking out the church. "And you are… some kind of immortal H.H. Holmes? Is that right?"

"Holmes was an amateur," Braham said. "But you're more or less correct."

"That's pretty awesome you can't die," Jojo said, still sounding like he was talking to an old friend. "That's a useful little trick."

"I find it does come in handy," Braham responded.

"Okay, you guys have got to be kidding me," I said, having enough of their weird exchange. "Are we going to keep dancing around the subject all day?"

Both men looked at me with completely straight faces.

"She's right," Jojo finally said. "I have to know… is that collar uncomfortable? I've always wondered."

"You get used to it after a while," Braham answered with a nod. "And it helps people trust you, so there's that."

"Smart," Jojo said.

"I'm going to die again because I'm surrounded by children." I sighed.

"That's not a nice thing for my favorite to say, Jane," Jojo said before turning to Braham. "You were right about that, by the way. She's definitely my favorite."

Braham nodded. "It wasn't hard to figure out."

"But on that note," Jojo said, finally giving me hope he was going to be useful. "I'm going to need you to let her go. HR will have a fit if I misplace one of my Boons. They're kind of sticklers about head count."

"I understand your concern, but I went through so much trouble to kill Jane and tie her to this box. I don't feel good about handing her over so easily," Braham said, pursing his lips. "If I give her back, how am I supposed to make a convenient little ghost army?"

"Why do you even want a ghost army to begin with?" Jojo asked. "Trust me, I've spent my entire afterlife trying to keep these guys in line. You'd be better off spending your immortality dominating the stock market or something. It's like herding cats. And not in a fun way."

"When is it ever fun to herd cats?" I asked, before mentally slapping myself on the forehead. "Never mind. I'm not encouraging this conversation."

I looked around the room, wondering if William had come back yet, but finding no sign of him. I tried to move but was still frozen in place, so he obviously hadn't found the spirit box yet. At least he hadn't destroyed it.

Hopefully, he was getting close, because if I was left alone with Jojo and Braham for too long, I worried I might lose my mind.

"Jojo, can you please just like... report him to the afterlife authorities or something?" I asked, before my eyes widened with a sudden idea. "Or banish him to Hell! Remember? You said you might be able to do that?"

"Oh right," Jojo said with a slow nod. "I forgot about that. Worth a try, I guess."

Jojo looked over at Braham, who seemed entirely unconcerned by the notion he might suddenly be banished to Hell. Instead, he sighed and looked at his watch.

Jojo took a deep breath and then flexed his entire body with a grunt, but nothing happened. "Hmmm. Well, that's embarrassing," Jojo said. "Performance anxiety."

He tried again, this time flexing harder, but still nothing happened.

"Sorry, Jane. I don't think I can banish people to Hell."

I groaned. "I'm so screwed."

"Jane! This is a church," Jojo said with an incredulous little gasp. "Have some respect."

"It's fine," Braham responded. "I'm sort of a priest, and I'll allow it."

"Thank you, Father," Jojo said, before continuing. "Now, I really have to ask you one more time to give me dear Jane back. I have a performance review coming up, and this won't look great."

"You know what, Jane, you're right. He does get old fast,"

Braham said, watching me intently for a moment before I collapsed onto the floor.

It felt like every single nerve in my body was on fire, and I writhed in pain, screaming out desperately.

"Stop!" I begged, feeling like my brain was pushing against my skull.

In an instant, Jojo was beside me on the ground. He kneeled over me and placed his hand on my forehead with genuine concern in his eyes.

"Jojo, please. Please make him stop. I can't stand it," I whimpered, my entire body tensing at once like I was being electrocuted. "Please."

I could feel tears running down my cheeks and pooling in my ears as every single muscle in my body contorted. It felt like at any moment, all my bones would break.

Jojo stood from me and faced Braham, his eyes suddenly oozing black liquid down his cheeks. A wind picked up in the entire room, blowing dust and old papers around as the ground began to shake.

The sight was like something out of a nightmare. It was a complete night and day difference from the sweet Jojo I was so used to.

"Let. Her. Go." Jojo's voice was deep and serious, and had I been in Braham's position, I would have given up right then and there.

But as I looked over at Braham, he didn't seem fazed in the slightest by Jojo's performance. If anything, he looked like he was watching an entertaining show.

"See, this is more like what I expected from you," Braham said with a gleeful little clap. "Much more impressive, Jojo."

"I won't ask you again," Jojo said, his voice still low. "Let Jane go."

Braham continued to smile, even in the middle of the chaos that whirled around him. He was like the calm eye of the hurricane.

"Why would I let her go when I'm finally getting a rise out of you?" Braham asked. "This is what I wanted from the beginning. If all I need to control the afterlife is a bit of torture, this will be much easier than I thought. You really are an emotional mess."

I bit back a scream as another wave of pain shot through my body. I didn't want to distract Jojo. He needed to take Braham down, and unfortunately, Braham was right. Jojo was too emotional. If he was too concerned about me, he wouldn't be able to do what needed to be done.

As if realizing this, Jojo calmed down, letting the winds die as his eyes returned to their normal honey brown.

"All right, fine. Let's try this a different way," Jojo said. "What exactly do you want? People like you usually have a list of demands, right?"

"Oh, honey, there's no one like me," Braham said with a pitying little smile as my pain lessened slightly.

"Of course. Because you're so unique. I almost forgot," Jojo said. "So then what does a unique and pioneering individual such as yourself want in a situation like this?"

Braham took a step closer to Jojo, meeting his eyes with an unwavering grin. "I already told you. I'd like control of your Boons."

"Right, I got that," Jojo said. "But why? So they can get you coffee and get your priest getup pressed?"

Braham kept his grin in place, but the corner of his eye twitched. "Don't mock me. And don't act like you're smarter than me."

Braham's voice was soft in the now-still church. The quiet stretched on for another moment before it was pierced by a high-pitched scream.

It took me a moment to realize I was the one screaming, but as the pain raged through my body once more, I only screamed louder.

As afterlives went, this one was really starting to suck.

I tried to look over to Jojo to see how he'd react to this latest wave of agony Braham was putting me through, but I couldn't manage to open my eyes. Every nerve was screaming.

And then I felt a hand on my shoulder.

"Jane!"

William. He had to have gotten the box if he was back here. Otherwise, what would be the point?

I forced my eyes open. He desperately scanned me, as if he might find the source of my pain written on my face.

As I screamed out, his eyes turned dark. But not just dark. Black.

He adopted the same eerie black eyes Jojo had had only a moment before. But this didn't look like it was for show. This was a genuine mask of rage contorting William's beautiful face into something terrifying.

His dark brows knitted together as he set his jaw firmly. Black veins sprang to life over his pale skin as he turned his lifeless eyes to Braham, manifesting on the spot.

"Who's this now?" Braham asked, looking genuinely confused.

William didn't bother answering. Instead, he yelled something in what I could only assume was Latin, before lifting the spirit box high over his head and smashing it against the stone floor, breaking it into a million little pieces.

Chapter 28

The second the box hit the ground, the pain stopped. I collapsed against the cold stone floor, feeling like I wanted nothing more than to pass out right then and there.

Almost immediately, William's light blue eyes returned, and the veins disappeared from his skin. He gathered me into his arms, encircling me safely against his chest.

"I'm here," he whispered over and over again, kissing the top of my head.

"Well done, William," Jojo said, his voice much too even for the incredibly dramatic half hour we'd just had. He even leaned over to Braham as he pointed at us and said, "I set them up. I'm kind of a matchmaker."

Had I not been so traumatized from the worst pain I'd ever felt in my afterlife, I would have rolled my eyes. As it was, I buried my face against William and breathed him in as he held me.

It was like breathing after nearly drowning.

"I know you," Braham said as he watched us. His eyes lit up at the sight of William. "Oh, this is too poetic. You're the git from the boat. The one who proposed. You were my first kill."

William looked at Braham with that same terrifying intensity he'd shown only a moment before, but as he moved to stand, I grabbed his arm.

"Stop. He's trying to get a rise out of you," I whispered. "And I need you."

William instantly broke eye contact with Braham to look back to me, the intensity melting into concern.

It was amazing the way he could flip that switch. I'd had no idea William could be so intimidating. That only made it that much more satisfying he was currently the person holding me. He was my protector.

"I'm glad you finally found someone who actually loves you," Braham said. "Sorry about what's-her-name."

William tensed against me, but he didn't make a move toward Braham. He stayed beside me, encircling me in his embrace. Just like I needed him to.

"I feel like this would be a good moment to point out you no longer control Jane," Jojo said. "And that you're trapped in a room with three very angry ghosts."

Braham nodded in an unconcerned way. "I may not have Jane tethered to the spirit box, but she'll always be tethered to me in some way. I killed her. That's just how it works."

"I must have missed that day in my afterlife training class," Jojo said. "But in any case, I wouldn't be quite so cocky if I were you."

"I know, Jojo," Braham said. "And that's why you're not me. Have you already forgotten I can't die?"

"You may not be able to die," Jojo began. "But think about how boring your eternity is going to be with every Boon, Guardian, Kin, and Beguiler keeping tabs on you? I can make sure they make your life miserable."

Braham grinned. "I would hope so. I love having an audience for my work. Unlike you, I don't have performance anxiety. Knowing I'm being watched makes it that much better."

"Mate, I don't think you understand. The whole point I'm making is we'll stop you at every turn," Jojo said. "I thought you were supposed to be the genius here."

Braham's smile faltered only slightly. "You can try. But you don't have the resources to stop me. Or the stomach."

"Listen, I may be as pretty as an angel, but that doesn't mean I am one."

"Jojo, that's a line from an *Avengers* movie." I groaned.

He pursed his lips. "Is it? I swear I came up with that."

"You didn't," I assured him. "Watching TV and movies is basically my only hobby in the afterlife."

"I stand by what I said," Jojo said, turning back to Braham. "I may not be able to kill you, but as Jane can attest, I'm very annoying when I want to be."

"It's true," I said, now standing up with help from William. "I've only been around Jojo for twenty years, and I'm already fed up with him. I can't imagine having him purposefully bugging me for all of eternity."

"Thanks, Jane," Jojo said, as if I'd just given him the best compliment I possibly could. "I'm a master at my craft."

Before Braham could answer, "Shake It Off" by Taylor Swift rang out in the echo-y church.

We all looked at each other in confused silence for a moment before Braham winced. "So sorry. Just one minute."

He pulled his cell phone out and held it up to his ear, turning away from us even though we could still easily hear him.

"Hey, Peach. What's going on?" He paused before looking over his shoulder at the group of ghosts silently waiting for him to finish his call. "No, nothing important. What's up?"

I looked over at Jojo with a shake of my head, but he just shrugged.

"Well, what did you do to her?" he asked the anonymous person on the other line. "I don't think erasing her memory is that harsh. She did kill your mother." Braham nodded a few more times. "Yeah, of course. Do whatever you need to do."

Braham placed his hand over the phone before mouthing, "Sorry" at us.

Jojo held up his hand in understanding.

"Yeah, Peach. I can be there soon. No, no. Don't worry about it. Concord isn't far. I've got a jet. Yeah, I'll see you in a minute. Bye."

Braham hung up and placed his phone back in his pocket, straightening his priest collar.

"Sorry about that. So rude, I know. But I've got to get going. Have something of a mess to sort out."

"You're not leaving," I said, glaring at Braham.

"Listen, Jane. I know we'll be seeing more of each other soon since... you know... I own you and everything. But now isn't the time," Braham said. "I'll catch you on the flip side."

Braham gave Jojo a little nod before turning a grin on William and me, taking a piece of pink bubble gum from his pocket, and popping it into his mouth. And with that, he walked out of the church.

"Seriously, Jojo? You're just going to let him walk away?" William asked. "He's killed people. He admitted it. He killed Jane!"

"And you," I pointed out.

"And me! We can't let him walk out of here."

"Wait Braham, come back," Jojo said halfheartedly. When the hot priest didn't return to the abandoned church, he gave us a shrug.

"That's it? That was your entire attempt to stop him?" I asked. "You're the leader of the Boons. You're a force of nature! You're Akahata! The Supreme One. How can you let a serial killer just walk away?"

"You're definitely better than this," William agreed.

Jojo pulled a guilty face at William's words. "I know this looks bad, but... my hands are sort of tied. What am I supposed to do if he can't die?"

We mulled this over in silence, our powerless position becoming more and more apparent.

"No, guys, I'm serious. What am I supposed to do? I'm asking you," Jojo said. "I have no idea."

"How am I supposed to know?" I asked. "I didn't even know the rules of the afterlife because *someone* never told me."

"You realize I did that on purpose, right?" Jojo said, seeming to forget about the fact that a violent psychopath had escaped from our custody.

I sighed. I wanted to point out how urgent it was that we stop Braham, but something told me that Jojo had already given up on thwarting him tonight.

"Yeah, you've said that, but you never actually explained why."

"The second I met you, I could tell you had the natural instinct to be a Boon. And I thought maybe you'd make a good second in command," Jojo said.

He'd definitely moved on from Braham already. This man had the worst attention span I'd ever seen.

"You want me to be your assistant?" I asked.

"Not like that. I'm not going to make you get coffee, unless you get really good coffee."

"Never going to happen," I said, cutting Jojo off before he could turn me into a coffee runner.

"Right. But anyway, I could use some help keeping everyone in control, and I thought you'd make a good candidate. I didn't tell you anything because I wanted to see how your instincts treated you in this whole thing."

I narrowed my eyes. "That's the thinnest excuse for inconveniencing someone so drastically that I've ever heard."

Jojo winced. "Yeah, I could have thought this plan through a bit better. But look at you! You've done so well."

I shook my head. "This isn't important right now, Jojo. We have to figure out what to do about Braham. We can't just let him leave."

"You're right. We need to find out if you're really tethered to him, because if that's true, then there's a higher up who's been keeping *me* in the dark."

"I think the first order of business should be to get Jane out of this drafty old church and back to her home. She's been through enough these past few weeks," William said, placing his arm protectively around me.

"Weeks?" I asked incredulously. "I was gone for weeks?"

"Didn't you know?" William asked, his voice all concern.

"I kind of lost track of time. Everything was so fuzzy when I was tethered to that box."

"The important thing is that we found you," William said, giving my arm a little squeeze.

I looked over at Jojo who was staring at the two of us with a dopey grin. I groaned at him. "What, Jojo?"

"You two," he said simply, gesturing to William and me. "I can't believe I actually managed to matchmake my two favorite Boons. I love it when a plan comes together."

"All right, we'll meet you at the Ramona house," I said, cutting him off. I didn't need him making things with William any more awkward than they already were.

"You're no fun," Jojo said. "It's not very often I get to see the fruits of my labors, and now you want to take that away from me."

"Fine," I said, standing up on my tiptoes and pressing my lips against William's briefly. I pulled away as quickly as I'd kissed him.

"Happy?" I asked, trying to play it cool even though my knees wanted to shake from our short kiss.

Jojo let out a little squeal of delight. "Thank you." He grinned before trying to adopt a serious face. "Okay, I'm going to head over to the stuffy Guardian headquarters in New York and put out an APB on a British sociopath."

"Psychopath," I corrected.

"Yeah, that," he agreed. "We may not be able to stop Braham alone, but if we've got the entire afterlife keeping an eye on him, I don't like his chances of keeping up his shady lifestyle."

"Sounds like a plan," I said. It wasn't a perfect resolution, but it was something.

Jojo gave me one last little salute, and I returned the gesture before he disappeared and I pulled myself and William away from the old church.

Chapter 29

The abandoned house in Ramona, California was empty. Or, I guess, emptier than normal. Jenny was making herself scarce on purpose.

I had to talk to her as soon as she got back to let her know it wasn't her fault Braham had tricked her. He'd been talking to Boons and killing people to get to Jojo for decades. He was a master at what he did. It wasn't her fault she hadn't seen through him.

William stood beside me in the living room with his hand still in mine from our travel. I could have let it go, but I wasn't quite ready to yet. I'd been touch-starved for twenty years before I met William. Then I'd been trapped in a literal box for weeks with no outside contact. I wasn't letting him go until he asked.

"It's quiet in here," William said, his voice low.

It sounded like he wasn't sure what we should talk about and was trying to make small talk. But that was okay; I knew what needed to be said.

"William, I'm so sorry," I said, turning to face him while still keeping my hands in his. "I lied to you. A lot. I told you I wasn't talking to Brody anymore when I was helping him with his idiotic plan."

"Jane, you don't need to do this," he said, pursing his lips.

"No, I really do. I spent all that time in that dumb box

worrying I'd never see you again. I thought that our last interaction would be you looking at me like I'd betrayed you."

"I don't know that you really promised me you wouldn't see Brody. I just sort of assumed," he said. "You didn't betray me." He was being entirely too understanding.

"Technicalities don't matter," I said. "I implied I wouldn't be seeing Brody anymore. You knew from the beginning there was something up with him. You tried to warn me, and I didn't listen."

William sighed, a slight sadness passing over him. "It hurt when I saw Brody there," he admitted. "I was so angry you'd brought him. And I thought I'd have time for us to fight about it. But when you disappeared, my anger did, too. I just wanted you back."

"But you were right to be angry. Brody was working for Braham the entire time," I said with a frown. "I'm so so sorry I led him to our special place. Even as I was doing it, I knew it didn't feel right."

William looked at our interlocked fingers and let a ghost of his incredible smile creep over his lips as his disappointment vanished. "Our special place," he repeated. "I like that."

My own smile appeared at his low voice. "I feel like I need to overwrite any bad memories of what happened in the bamboo forest with Brody."

Now William's small smile broke into a full dimple-making grin.

He was devastatingly handsome.

"And how are you going to overwrite those memories?" he asked.

His voice did that thing where it went from low to impossibly deep, and goosebumps erupted all over my body.

"I have ideas," I whispered, pressing my lips to his for the briefest of moments.

I smiled as I moved away. William let his hands slide over my waist and around to my back, pulling me to him with that devilish grin that made my knees buckle. Luckily, he held me against him to stop me from passing out right then and there.

"I was utterly broken when you went missing," he whispered, touching his nose to mine and closing his eyes. "I've been alone for so long, Jane. Longer than I care to admit. And a lot of that was by choice."

I could feel his breath against my lips as he spoke. My body was in a battle against my brain. I wanted to hear what he had to say, but I also wanted to kiss him again.

"I've never met someone I connect with like you. Which is humorous, when you think about how different we are," he said, giving my nose a little nudge with his own. "But my afterlife is better with you in it. That's all there is to it."

I smiled. "I really don't want to like you the way I do, just because I don't want to give Jojo the satisfaction of knowing he was right," I said. "But he was. Totally and completely."

"Totally and completely," William agreed with a nod, before he closed the space between us.

His lips brushed mine in a soft, slow kiss. It was easy and relaxed as I pulled him more firmly against me.

I wanted to be enveloped by him forever.

The kiss deepened gradually, as if we had all the time in the world; his lips moved slowly and deliberately over mine as his hands trailed up my back.

Even with the slow pace of the kiss, my entire body felt like it was on fire. It was incredible the way he could instantly heighten every sensation I felt with just one touch.

"Hey," I whispered against his lips, pulling away just enough to look into his piercing blue eyes. "I totally love you."

He laughed softly at this, that devastating smile back in place. "Only you could make the word 'totally' sound romantic," he said. "It's one of the many reasons I totally love you, too."

My breath caught in my chest. I'd thought he would say it back. I'd hoped he would. But I wasn't positive.

I pulled him to me once more, giving him what I hoped would be the best kiss of his afterlife. He responded by tangling his fingers in my hair and kissing me back as if this was the first in a long afterlife full of kisses.

This was even better than when Paul Rudd kissed Alicia Silverstone at the end of *Clueless*. That's how perfect it was.

Plus, William wasn't my ex-step-brother… so there was that.

I wanted to kiss him for all of eternity. And I probably would have, but Jojo's familiar voice suddenly entered the room.

"I'm knocking! I'm here! I'm coming into the room," he said loudly, before entering the living room with his hand dramatically over his eyes. "Is everyone decent?"

If I wasn't dead, I would have blushed.

"Worst timing I've ever seen, mate," William said, catching me off guard.

"Feeling hostile, are we, William?" Jojo asked.

"I was a bit busy," William emphasized, still embracing me.

I rested my head against William's chest. "It's okay. We have an entire afterlife of Jojo interruptions ahead of us.

Chapter 30

The sunset from the Hollywood sign was one of my favorite things. Not only because I was pretty sure it would make an amazing album cover if I ever got Jojo to start a band with me, but because it looked out over an entire city of people who had no idea we were hanging out up there.

Sure, the air was full of pollution, and the faint sounds of sirens wafted toward us on the breeze, but it was home. And it was way better than some stuffy old spirit box.

"Guys, I legit will never be able to apologize enough for not knowing the hot priest was a literal psychopath," Jenny said for the millionth time.

Apparently, almost getting me enslaved by a lunatic had turned her penitent. She wouldn't stop apologizing, no matter how many times we told her it was fine.

"In my defense though, his face was like, an actual Greek statue… but hotter," she went on. "Like, I have never in all my years of life and death seen someone so gorgeous."

"Can we stop talking about how attractive a serial killer is?" I asked. "Even for my true crime junkie side, it's a bit much."

I sat beside William in the middle of the Hollywood "H" with Jojo and Jenny on the other side of me.

Our legs dangled high above the air as a slight breeze picked up.

"She's not wrong though," Jojo said.

"I thought you were all in love with some peach-haired witch," I reminded him. "Isn't she your great love or something?"

Jojo clutched invisible pearls like I'd betrayed some deep trust. "Don't say that like she and I won't end up together, you love killer."

"Jojo, she doesn't even know you exist."

"And I'll fix that... one day," he said.

"It's so peculiar to see Jojo nervous about talking to a girl." William laughed, his fingers laced through mine. "I never thought I'd see the day."

"Staaaahp," Jojo whined. "I'm thinking up the best way to introduce myself."

"And what have you come up with?" I asked.

At my question, Jojo sat up straighter, a grin forming on his face. "Okay, so get this. I'm going to appear in her bathroom mirror one day all covered in blood and be like, 'do you want to know how you're going to die? Because you've been killing me for years.' And then I'll like... turn the blood into glitter... or flowers... or something equally romantic."

Jenny groaned at this idea without ever looking up from her useless phone. "That is the actual worst idea I've ever heard."

Jojo beamed, as if he hadn't heard her. "It's going to be perfect."

I shook my head, not wanting to be the one to break the news to Jojo that his plan was more full of holes than the hot priest's grasp on religion. "You'll do great, Jojo."

"See? Jane believes in me!" Jojo said, giving me an appreciative smile. "It's hard to be true romantics surrounded by cynics, isn't it, dear Jane?"

"So hard," I agreed dramatically as I leaned my head against William's shoulder.

He kissed the top of my head, and I tried not to beam like a dopey, lovesick puppy.

"Jojo, how exactly did the hot priest talk to me and stuff if he isn't dead?" Jenny asked after a moment.

"Braham," I corrected.

Yes, he was sort of a priest and yes, he was hot, but calling him Hot Priest felt like he was a good guy. And Braham was so obviously a villain.

"Hot Priest is kind of immortal in a weird way," Jojo explained, totally ignoring my attempt to call him by his real name. "No one really seems to know what he is. I'm not sure he even knows what he is. He's the only person the leaders have ever met who didn't die."

"Oh great. So, there's an immortal psychopath on the loose trying to figure out how to control the afterlife," I said, my voice heavy with sarcasm.

"Don't worry, Jane," Jojo began. "Now that everyone in the afterlife is aware of him, Braham won't be able to sneeze without someone being alerted."

I raised my eyebrows at Jojo. "Really? Because you look pretty relaxed right now. Not exactly the high-alert watchdog you're promising me."

"Oh well, not *me*. I'm not going to be following him. I've got too much important stuff to do," he said, very unconvincingly. "But other, more qualified people are keeping an eye on him."

Jojo flashed me a wide grin as he chewed his wad of bubblegum.

Why didn't his words reassure me at all?

"Oh!" he suddenly exclaimed. "I almost forgot. Given recent... happenings..."

"Jane getting kidnapped by a psychopath and enslaved?" William clarified.

Jojo pointed at him with a nod. "Yeah, that. Given that whole situation, I've decided we need a better way to keep in contact with each other in case there's ever another emergency."

I furrowed my brow, wondering what in the word Jojo could be talking about. Before I could ask, he pulled four cell phones out of the pocket of his purple plaid suit coat.

"Are those what I think they are?" I asked, looking at the

phones in confusion.

It took all of two seconds for Jenny to look up from her nonfunctioning phone and take in the sight before her.

"Jojo," she whispered, almost reverently. "Are you giving me a phone?"

"Do those even work in the afterlife?" I asked.

"If everyone would stop asking questions and give me two seconds to talk," Jojo said pointedly. "These are some cell phones I rigged to work for the four of us. That means you can't tell the other Boons because they'd be pissed."

"I swear," Jenny said automatically, holding her fingers up like a boy scout.

"Also, you're on the afterlife plan, which means no social media and no texting living people. I'm looking at you, Jenny," he emphasized, giving her a stern look while she held out her grabby hands for the phone.

"Just give it to me please," she whined, dragging the last word out in a nasally high-pitched voice. "This is literally the only thing I've wanted since I died."

"Jenny," Jojo said again, his voice stern. "No texting living people."

"I won't, I swear. Just hand it over."

Jojo gave Jenny the phone before handing one to me and William as well. William looked at it in utter confusion.

"Don't worry, your girlfriend will explain it to you," Jojo said with a wink.

"Yeah, nice try, but I have no idea how to work this thing either," I said, staring at the thin rectangle.

"I'll get that snake game loaded up on there to make it less scary for you," Jojo promised. "And I'm sure Jenny would be more than happy to give you two a tutorial on... what is happening?"

Jojo looked down at his phone, that was now pinging as if an alarm was going off. He frowned at the screen.

"Jenny, why am I getting an alert that you've already made several social media profiles?" Jojo asked. "And you posted?

Are you kidding me?"

"Just had to let that skank Remy know I know she started dating my ex right after I died," Jenny said, concentrating on her screen as her thumbs flew across it. "Guess who's back—"

Jojo took Jenny's phone away before she could finish her sentence, though I was pretty sure I knew how it ended.

"Jenny!" Jojo exclaimed, looking down at her phone. "Are you kidding me right now? You're trending on social media! People are saying a vigilante ghost is back from the dead to spill the tea."

"I miss tea so much." William sighed beside me.

"Remy knows what she did," Jenny said with a shrug, looking completely unconcerned with the mess she'd just made.

"How did you start trending in less than five minutes?" Jojo asked, looking genuinely concerned for his job stability right at that moment.

"Girl, I told you. I am a legend. You should have seen me when I was alive," she said, sounding proud as she gave Jojo a satisfied smirk.

"Unbelievable," he muttered.

It felt kind of nice to see Jojo having to deal with an adult child the way I always had to deal with him. It was good for him to get a taste of his own medicine from time to time.

"That's it. I'm revoking your phone privileges, young lady," he said, putting the phone into his purple plaid pocket.

"You can't do that," Jenny whined.

"Too late. I'm leaving. You can't have it back," Jojo said, just as Jenny reached out for him.

In an instant, they were both gone, Jojo accidentally taking Jenny with him wherever he'd disappeared to.

"Glad I don't have to be there for that fight," I said with a laugh.

"Agreed. I'm not sure who's scarier: Jojo having to actually do his job for once, or Jenny without a phone." William smiled with that gorgeous smile that engulfed his entire face.

"Geez, you're beautiful," I said without really meaning to. I would have been embarrassed, but he already knew how smitten I was. There was no playing it cool anymore.

His grin grew. "I'm so glad that you have no pretense. It's... refreshing."

"I think that's a nice way of saying I have no poker face," I teased, leaning in to him. "But I'm serious. My afterlife was kind of a drag before you got here. I'm just... I'm glad you're here."

William leaned over and kissed me softly. It was brief, but it was perfection.

When he pulled away, my own grin formed as a thought hit me.

"I had no idea how terrifying you could be until I saw you with Braham," I said, a plan beginning to take shape in my mind. "That was seriously scary."

William looked embarrassed by my praise. "That side of me has literally never come out before. I didn't even really know it was there. But I couldn't handle the thought of him hurting you."

"Oh, you don't need to be embarrassed. It was oddly attractive," I said, garnering a surprised look from William. "The reason I bring it up is because I ran into this bratty teenager not too long ago who kept making fun of me for not being a scary ghost."

I let my words trail off as I gave William a meaningful look.

"Any chance my terrifying new boyfriend could do me a solid and scare the snark out of a teenager for me?"

William blessed me with his devastating smile once more before he answered.

"I would be absolutely delighted, darling."

Acknowledgements

My writer's group has been completely and totally vital in my writing career. Without them, I would have let imposter syndrome take over long ago. Thank you so much to Heather Pead and Lisa Harris. Your enthusiasm for Jojo's ridiculousness and our long therapy sessions kept me going!

Thank you to my husband, who doesn't get too scared whenever an author in a movie decides to murder their spouse. I know you've noticed how often that happens. Thanks for sticking with me anyway. Sovay, Link, and Salem, thank you for giving mom a few seconds of peace each day to write. And thank you for your endless imagination that helps me keep seeing the magic in even the smallest thing.

Mom and Dad, thanks for loving movies and video games so I could become the giant nerd I am today.

Allison and Jenna, thanks for sticking with me, even though I STILL haven't released the third Parrish book. Your kind words have kept me going more often than you both know.

And to my readers, you guys are the actual best. I'm sorry I'm so inconsistent with release dates. But thank you for being along for the ride.

About the Author

Shannen Camp is a California-born writer who loves ghosts, gaming, and miniature schnauzers. Her fifteen YA and New Adult novels cover almost every genre, but always have to have some sort of romance; even when all the characters are technically dead. Shannen now lives in Utah with her husband, three kids, and three miniature schnauzers. While writing will always be her first love, Shannen is also studying to become a Mortician, to the surprise of absolutely no one.
You can find Shannen's published works on Amazon and connect with her on social media @AuthorShannenCamp

More from this author

Made in the USA
Columbia, SC
09 November 2023

25833765R00117